TALES IN A MINOR KEY

PETER FREUND

ISBN: 1468040383
ISBN-13: 9781468040388
Library of Congress Control Number: 2012900036

CreateSpace, North Charleston, SC

CONTENTS

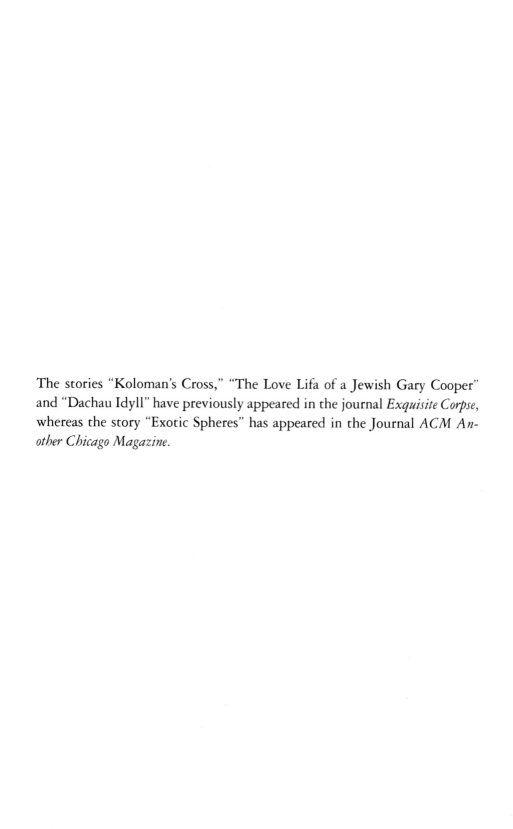

The stories "Koloman's Cross," "The Love Lifa of a Jewish Gary Cooper" and "Dachau Idyll" have previously appeared in the journal *Exquisite Corpse,* whereas the story "Exotic Spheres" has appeared in the Journal *ACM Another Chicago Magazine.*

THE ALDERMAN'S BONDS

The railings flanking the worn marble staircase have not been replaced in over a century. Their current heavily varnished gray, or maybe off-white, appearance conceals many an earlier coat of paint. Here and there the paint has chipped off, as have the coats hidden under it. A careful inspection of the left railing near its top reveals a hole, at the bottom of which a keen eye cannot miss the original gold leaf in which this railing was covered in 1878 when the Palace of Culture opened. The now dirty oft re-plastered walls were painted white in those days and all the detailing was in gold leaf as well, giving the lobby a baroque splendor, which set the mood as one climbed to the hall with its ornate sunroof and huge crystal chandeliers.

Supposedly built for chamber music concerts in a wing jotting out from the much more sumptuous opera house, this Palace of Culture was in reality intended to house the many balls with which society chased away boredom and melancholy in a city engaged in the wholesale and retail wheat trade. Though technically part of Hungary, Temesvár, as it was then called, housed an Austrian garrison. It was after all the capital of the Banat and the revenues from this granary of the Empire flowed directly into the privy purse of the Habsburgs, who wanted the region free of flare-ups of Hungarian nationalism.

The 1899 ball season started early and was meant to culminate later on in the New Century Ball. On a mid-October Saturday the merchants in black tails, escorting their ladies with rolled-up hairdos wearing ivory colored dresses, started arriving shortly after ten. They dropped their wraps at the *garderobe*, and then ceremoniously headed for their reserved tables in

1

the hall. At eleven sharp the portly mayor mounted the podium at the far end of the hall and was seated on a gilded antique-looking armchair upholstered in red silk. The twenty-man City Council then joined him and remained standing. The orchestra started on *Gott erhalte* and one and all rose to pay homage to the beloved Habsburg Emperor, the sponsor of all this prosperity. After the anthem, the two aldermen closest to the mayor stretched a blue silk ribbon in front of His Honor, which he then proceeded to cut with a pair of gold-plated scissors removed without accident from his pants' pocket. Like a bridge, the 1899 Temesvár ball season was thus declared open. The cotillion formed and the flower of Temesvár youth started the dancing.

At one table along the outer wall sat the Weinberg family, Joseph, Sidi, their two sons and a teen beauty wearing the only dark green silk dress at this ball. Green was passé, ivory was in, but if this obviously provincial girl dressed out of fashion, she could afford to do so. Her beauty was so marked that she needed neither makeup nor jewels to enhance it. Her bearing was noble, she was not tall but perfectly proportioned. She appeared charmingly modest and not in the least off-putting. The attention she attracted was rivaled only by that lavished on alderman Armin Fein who at the conclusion of the opening ceremony joined his mistress Kató Ligeti at a table he and his brother Maxi, the gynecologist, had reserved. The thirtyish alderman, close to six feet tall, walking tense like an officer in uniform, cut a handsome figure, his receding hairline compensated by his polished rigid mustache extending beyond his mouth and ending in a curl on either side. A prosperous wheat merchant, Armin Fein was the most eligible bachelor in town, and on this gala occasion — with all the marriageable daughters in Temesvár bedecked with all the diamonds their mothers could spare — had the gall to show up with Kató Ligeti who, for money mind you, was known to have slept with every able-bodied male in town, and now was sleeping with Armin for free, supposedly "for the fun of it". It was worse than bad taste, it was a regular scandal, as all the ladies agreed.

Sidi Weinberg played it safe and admonished Aranka Ausländer, her pretty niece from Losonc, the one in the dark green silk dress, not to glance even furtively at the wicked alderman, for reasons on which she did not wish to elaborate. Overwhelmed by the opulence of the occasion, Aranka Ausländer may not even have noticed the eligible bachelor with the polished mustache and his mistress of ill repute. Aunt Sidi's admonishment kindled her curiosity and she started throwing a few furtive glances in the alderman's direction, then some more, until she ended up staring at him outright.

The two Weinberg boys and Joseph took turns dancing with their out-of-town relative, and what with all that staring, at some point even the proud alderman took notice of Aranka. When least expected, at least by Aunt Sidi, the free alderman — Kató Ligeti had just been asked for a dance by an "old flame" — appeared at the Weinberg table and to everyone's consternation asked Aranka Ausländer to waltz with him. The musicians followed this waltz by another, then by a polka with gallop, then with a slower piece to give the dancers a breather. During this slow dance Armin Fein's face came close enough to that of his partner, for the right curl of his mustache to tickle her right cheek. They both burst out laughing, at first awkwardly, then with zest. Armin Fein now looked into Aranka Ausländer's eyes, pulled her body close to his and for the first time ever impressed on her what it means to be a man. Presently the music stopped, the alderman returned his partner to the Weinberg table, clicked his heels, bowed, kissed her hand and returned to his own table.

Kató Ligeti was visibly annoyed, Sidi Weinberg was outright furious. If she didn't shout at her niece, it was solely because she didn't wish to create a scene with all the attendant *blamage*. She contented herself with pursing her lips and in the coldest tone available to her, whispering to the girl who had just gotten her first intimation of ecstasy, "You are going back to Losonc, first thing tomorrow morning. Now it's time to go home", it was barely past midnight. With eyes darting anger at Aranka she added, "You ruined this evening for me, wait till your mother hears of this".

According to Ausländer family lore, while her niece disgraced the family with a known *roué* on the dancing floor at the opening of the 1899 Temesvár ball season, Sidi Weinberg sweat through her Vienna-made silk dress, had a dizzy spell, fainted and had to be discreetly revived with smelling salts. Of course this part of the Ausländer legend elicits laughter from all, for the story is a funny one, and it looked like it had a happy ending.

The next morning Sidi personally put Aranka on the first train to Losonc and handed her a sealed envelope to be delivered to her mother upon arrival. Had Sidi but waited a few more hours, she could have avoided the role of laughable villain in this story, for at noon Alderman Armin Fein called at the Weinberg residence on Kossuth Square, a five-minute walk from the *Fabrikstadt* synagogue. He handed Sidi a bouquet of pink carnations and wished to talk to her beautiful niece. Sidi hemmed and hawed. Though still angry with the girl, the meaning of this formal visit by the town's most eligible bachelor was not lost on Sidi, so she invented something about a telegram urgently recalling her niece to Losonc.

"She is from Losonc?" inquired the eager alderman.

"Yes, very good family I might add" by which she simply meant "they are related to us." But all this did not register with the mustachioed alderman, he was in love, it was written all over his face, he was willing to travel to Losonc, to the end of the world if need be, to claim his Cinderella.

A week later, following arrangements made by Sidi with the preface "ignore my letter", Armin Fein showed up at the Ausländer house in the center of Losonc. Mr. Ausländer was in the textile business and did modestly well. The Ausländers were impressed by Sidi's recommendation "Armin Fein is a very successful wheat trader, he is an alderman, need I say more? After all these years my Joseph has never even been invited to attend a City Council session."

The gentleman caller was treated to a festive lunch at the Losonc house. Seated between Mrs. Ausländer and her old mother, the Temesvár alderman could behold his beloved, a few feet away from him. She kept her eyes lowered for the better part of the elaborate meal, but a few times their eyes did meet and beams of desire flashed across the heavy black dining room table covered in finest damask cloth. The focal point of this table was its other end whence Mr. Ausländer held forth. One spoke only if asked. In case of need, one could gain the floor by repeated discreet coughing. Anyway, except for the paterfamilias, the other diners concentrated much of the time on the exquisite meal, from the tomato soup with egg dumplings, through the *ráczos hal,* tender carp roasted Serbian style on a bed of crisp potato and onion slices, smothered in sour cream and spiked here and there with smoked bacon — this household wasn't kosher observed Armin Fein, to his relief. A fine chilled *Szürke Barát* was served to wash down the fish and a cherry *strudel* followed by a glass of Tokay concluded the meal in style. The gentlemen then retired to the salon of this heavy Victorian house and there, over Havana cigars, Armin Fein asked Mr. Ausländer for the hand of his daughter.

This was obviously not unexpected, yet the proud father called in Aranka and, lest he appear tyrannical, asked her for her consent, which the girl gave without the slightest hesitation. The wedding was scheduled for December, the last Nineteenth Century wedding in the Ausländer family. The dowry of the Losonc beauty was meager, but the groom was well to do. When standing side by side under the *chuppah* their hands touched ever so slightly, sending a *frisson* through both bride and groom. This was a marriage made in heaven, or so it seemed.

Alderman Fein attended the New Century Ball in the company of his radiant young wife, now wearing an ivory colored silk dress like all the other ladies. The dashing young couple was the focus of every lorgnon in the hall. The alderman let it be known that as of the first day of the new century he was resigning from the City Council to devote full attention to his wife and to his business. The former playboy was now spending his nights at home. The conjugal bed can be a very inviting place when both spouses wish to be in it.

By February 1901 they had a son Karl to show for all this and four years later a second son Ödön was born. It was true happiness. In 1907 Aranka became pregnant yet again, but Armin wanted no more children, they were too much of an intrusion on his happiness, they took up too much of Aranka's time, even with a nanny, a cook and a maid. Armin decreed that Aranka shall have an abortion. Though illegal in Catholic Austria-Hungary, an abortion was a viable option for a Jew, who anyway wasn't headed for the same region of Paradise as His Apostolic Majesty.

An abortion was to be performed by Armin's brother, Dr. Maxi Fein. Maxi lived in a villa standing on an empty field abutting the *Fabrikstadt* Synagogue. Though almost as tall as his brother, Maxi was corpulent and bald, sweat profusely and carried a big wart on his right cheek. Neither his shirtsleeves nor his fingernails were ever immaculate; he looked unkempt. Yet Maxi thrived as the abortionist of choice for many a socialite. The two brothers were not close; Maxi had settled in an unhappy marriage many years earlier and was inordinately jealous of his dashing younger brother. He relished having Armin come to him now for a favor. The operation would be free of charge of course, *en famille.* They agreed on a date in February right after Karl's sixth birthday.

The operation went smoothly, Maxi was assisted by his wife. After a few hours' rest Aranka and Armin were offered a smooth ride home in a *Gummirädler,* a horse drawn carriage with rubber-covered wheels. That night,

Aranka awoke covered in sweat, she was burning. Armin sent the maid for Maxi. An infection had set in, those dirty fingernails should have been assessed more carefully by the trusting couple.

"Do something!" Armin shouted at his brother.

"There's nothing I or anyone else can do"

"Let's take her to a hospital"

"Do you want to ruin me? Is that what I deserve? They can't do anything anyway, except make an autopsy and I'd end up in jail. All right, destroy your own brother simply because he was willing to help you, for free at that, ...mind you"

Just as the bells of the Catholic Cathedral near Kossuth Square started ringing noon, death paid a visit at the Haymarket, three blocks away, and the Fein family lost its only female member.

Armin jumped his brother and grabbed him by the throat, but the nanny and Resi, the maid, restrained him. Maxi could only mutter, "It's not my fault, it's not my fault."

Armin Fein cried the whole rest of the day, at night he was howling by his wife's corpse "Aranka I love you, I can't live without you."

The children, especially the six-year-old Karl, didn't know what to make of this, and, to tell the truth, Armin couldn't care less. In a sense he blamed them, it was a child, a would-be child that robbed him of the one dearest to him. The Fein household went into deep mourning, the official cause of death as certified by Dr. Maxi Fein was given as "salami poisoning," a nice Freudian flourish. Hundreds of people showed up at the funeral and it was clear to one and all that Armin had to remarry soon, lest he fall completely apart and the children be completely neglected. After the funeral Maxi came over and impressed upon his younger brother the importance of sticking to the "salami" story, "you are now an accessory, keep that in mind". Armin just nodded, he was in a daze.

A month later Sidi Weinberg, who had her own very serious doubts about the salami story, but was willing to avoid that sensitive topic, "it can't bring Aranka back to life", came over to Armin with a proposition, "I know how much you loved her" she patted his hand while Armin sat like a child, "But something must be done, you can't go on like this. It would be best for you to remarry and I know this young girl in Pozsony, decent family", she was obviously *not* a relative "It would be best for the children as well".

A burdened Armin Fein was put on a train for Pozsony by Sidi and a few friends.

Two days later he appeared at the Fink home, literally a house with three girls, Jozsa and Janka marriageable, and the eleven year old Franziska. The names of the girls clearly revealed the reverence the Finks accorded His Royal Imperial Majesty Franz Joseph. Armin was resigned and the father talked him into taking the eldest, Jozsa, off his hands. "We are poor folks," the Finks had a notions outlet in the old town "We cannot give you a dowry, but Jozsa will make you a good wife and we insist you take Janka along as well. The two of them will look after you and your sons." Armin had had paradise and lost it, the rest hardly mattered. The next day without much pomp Armin Fein married Jozsa Fink and the new couple accompanied by the bride's sister Janka headed for Temesvár.

Unlike her predecessor, Jozsa Fein, née Fink, was no beauty. A small heavy-set woman, friendly and full of good will, she was a hard worker, a responsible person. She mastered the household in a matter of days, and in that same short time the maid Resi, the nanny and the cook, became her respectful and willing staff. Jozsa knew she was not first choice, but at twenty-three years of age, she was happy to be a choice at all. She had all but resigned herself to spinsterhood when the Temesvár alderman came to fetch her. The transition to the new setting was smoothed over somewhat by the presence of Janka, Jozsa's squinting clone.

Jozsa took well to the children. With the two-year-old Ödön, this second wife suddenly found herself with a secondhand baby. All her love was lavished on this boy. Karl, the big one resented her as an intruder, an interloper, an usurper, but to Jozsa's mind that was to be expected and sooner or later he would come around as well. In fact it was later, much later, if ever.

Though aware that her primary duty in this household was that of a mother, Jozsa, a virgin, knew full well that further duties awaited her as Armin's wife. The first night in the bedroom Jozsa did her evening toiletries and then expectantly took occupancy of the right half of the solid oak matrimonial bed. Her husband joined her on his side and shortly thereafter started sliding over to her. Jozsa had been prepared by her mother to expect something of the sort. Armin touched her, kissed her and then his eyes took in Aranka's picture hanging on the wall by the foot of the bed. Armin sighed, he withdrew and then he fell asleep. Things did not take anything like the course Jozsa's mother had led her to expect.

Understandably, Jozsa assumed she had done something wrong. The next night the same interplay repeated itself and so it did for seven more nights in a row. After that Armin started finding excuses for staying out late. Jozsa wrote her mother whose reply contained a list of useful suggestions: spray perfume on the bed, let your husband see you while you undress, and other well-meaning stratagems. Trouble was, Armin was allergic to perfume and seeing Jozsa undress only exacerbated his longing for Aranka. Instead of her shapely body and rosy breasts he now was offered two big breasts hanging over a big belly. Instead of his first wife's lasciviously curving buttocks he now saw a well padded behind. Jozsa was quite unhappy and worried, not that she had intense sexual needs, it was more a matter of appearances, what will people say if she never had a child of her own. True, the two children that came with the deal were keeping her busy, but before long, tongues would start wagging.

Half a year into this stalemate, a sudden visit of the Losonc matriarch accompanied by Tuka, one of Aranka's sisters, was suddenly announced by Sidi Weinberg. Sidi's assurances notwithstanding, the Losonc family had conjured up scenarios of two defenseless little boys maltreated by a fairytale stepmother.

On a Monday morning the children's grandmother, protected from the sunshine by a frilly umbrella and backed up by her daughter rang the bell at the Haymarket apartment with as severe an expression on her face as she could place on it. A nervous Jozsa herself came to the green door. Between its spindles she got a first look at the woman who could be her damnation or salvation. The tension between Jozsa and her visitors resolved within minutes. One could not miss Jozsa's basic goodness and decency, no matter how biased one was to start with. Resi, the nanny and the cook backed up their mistress, from the heart, not out of a sense of duty.

After a tour of the apartment, in which very little had been changed since Aranka's time, the stern grandmother moved to tears by memories, her daughter Tuka, and her host sat down for coffee and cake in the salon. By the time they were stirring large sugar cubes into their strong coffees, a rapport, an incipient friendship had sprung up between them. When they finished eating, Jozsa called in Resi to clean up and then, as if on the spur of the moment, suggested that Tuka might want to take in the sights and odors of the Haymarket with Resi as her guide. Once alone with Mrs. Ausländer, slowly but deliberately, Jozsa started directing the conversation towards the nightly bedroom fiasco,

"I love it here and I am coming to grips with my duties while making sure that a loving and respectful memory of your daughter survives."

"I am sure you do, there's no doubt about it."

" I adore the children, little Ödön, if he were my own, I ..."

"I know."

"There is something you should be aware of, though." Jozsa Fink had realized that if anyone could remove the debilitating portrait from the bedroom, it would be the departed wife's own mother, so she went on, "Armin does not come close to me in bed"

"Really, you needn't ..."

"I mean he tries, but then he invariably ends up staring at your daughter's portrait and stops"

"What portrait?"

At this the two ladies just about jumped up from their comfortable seats and headed for the bedroom.

"That one" Jozsa pointed to the cause of her frustration.

"I see what you mean ... and you, out of respect ... oh, that portrait must go, into the ... dining room, yes the dining room" said Mrs. Ausländer as she embraced her grandchildren's stepmother. Jozsa Fink started crying bitterly. "It's all right, it's all taken care of now, don't cry ...my *daughter.*" Mrs. Ausländer emphasized her acceptance of the little chubby woman from Pozsony. She had learned to trust her. When Resi and the young Ausländer girl came back from the Haymarket, the portrait was moved into the dining room out of the line of sight of the seated Armin. The problem *was* solved. A year later little Erwin was born and at three sons the Fein family had achieved full size.

With his second wife Armin Fein did not take his conjugal duties as seriously as he had with Aranka. He let it be known that he was ready to rejoin the City Council and his wish was immediately granted. Armin Fein was an alderman again. Many an evening he spent at a card table at the Officers' Club next to the old City Hall. They played with Hungarian cards, their colorful suits marked in acorns, squashes, red and green, instead of the clubs, diamonds hearts and spades. Officers would dash in and out of the club, with floozies in tow. Now and then Armin himself would dine a shapely floozy or two in a *séparée* and end up spending the better part of the night in their company, like in his bachelor days. At home no one dared raise any questions, though in the morning Resi would direct a knowing look at her mistress and Jozsa would respond with a sustained sigh. That was however as far as these things went.

On the whole, the Haymarket residents enjoyed life in style, the wheat market was robust. They often took in an opera performance, more for its social aspects. Jozsa would follow the singers with her *lorgnon* while her husband would explore the bejeweled bosoms of young women with his. These young women in turn would eye Austrian officers not attached to floozies, it was quite a dynamic scene, very operatic. In all truth Jozsa much preferred operetta, above all that eternal Viennese kitsch *Drei Mäderl Haus*. Its score was a harmonically sanitized arrangement of Franz Schubert melodies. Its book concerned a wealthy Viennese businessman whose three daughters end up marrying three of that great Viennese composer's friends, while Franz himself remains unattached, not surprisingly, given that the good industrialist did not sire a son.

There is a moment when evening falls, all three daughters are gone, the house is empty and the lonely parents embark on a duet based on a melody from a string quartet. This invariably brought the house down, what with lyrics like "no more laughter, no more chatter, the fun is gone" which perfectly captured the range of pain conceivable to wheat merchants and their spouses. Yes, when everything is peaceful and life is good, comfortable parents get to miss their children. But life was not going to stay good much longer, His Royal-Imperial Majesty's days were numbered. Still at this point what the good burghers of Temesvár missed most was, in the words of the song, the laughter, the chatter, the fun of youth.

But then in the summer of 1914, all hell broke loose, everyone was declaring war on someone, it felt so good. His Royal Imperial Majesty declared war on the Serbs to avenge the death of His to Him insufferable nephew the Archduke Franz-Ferdinand. The Kaiser, not to be outdone, found his own Slav to fight, the Tsar himself. Then just to spread the fun around, he also declared war on France and attacked her through Belgium. This gave George V the opportunity to join the fray. This had its effects even on Temesvár's Haymarket. A war is no fun, even if they do battle elsewhere. After all, they could get bored and move the show closer to home. With America entering the war on the *other* side, nothing could be taken for granted any longer. What if the Serbs and the Italians, no further away than Trieste, were to invade Temesvár, what if? There was a Lloyd Triestino in Temesvár after all, but would they stop at reclaiming that? Of course they wouldn't, they'd loot the city. The City Council met to debate this very issue. And what was one to do? Be prudent, that's what, convert to assets both liquid and portable, diamonds in other words. But then who would want to convert everything to hard stones, their value always inflated at purchase, and subject to a hefty commission at sale. Diamonds may be forever as the saying goes, nothing else is *that* long lived, but then the Habsburgs come in a close second, and Armin Fein decided to convert all his assets to Royal-Imperial bonds bearing a facsimile of His Majesty's signature. So, the post-war world may be a little different, but there will always be a Habsburg Kaiser.

Well, who could have foreseen that not only would His Majesty meet His Maker, He was in His late seventies after all, but that He would take the whole monarchy with Him? Those bonds bearing His signature were not even usable in the toilet, the paper was too hard. At the end of the war, Armin Fein was wiped out, he had not a penny left to his name and a wheat wholesaler without a penny to his name, though not an ox and not a moron, is at the very least an oxymoron. Armin Fein was finished, kaput! He was nearing fifty, his eldest son a high school graduate, and he would have to start from scratch. This was too much for Armin Fein. He couldn't move one way or the other, he was in a state of total paralysis. He decided to retire. To *what,* and more importantly *on* what, was left unspecified. All that was crystal clear to Armin Fein, was that he absolutely *had* to retire. There was no alternative, or if there was one, he could not see it, and even had he been able to see it, he didn't *want* to.

With the Emperor went also the Empire. The Banat was divided into three parts, one part each for Hungary, Romania and the newly created Yugoslavia. Just who would get Temesvár, its capital, was up in the air for a few weeks. First the Serbs marched in, but then Queen Marie of Romania, the one in the Cole Porter song, journeyed to Versailles and when she demanded Temesvár she got it, you can't say no to a queen.

The Serbs marched out as fast as they had marched in, and Temesvár became Timişoara. This of course meant that the official language was

changed from Hungarian to Romanian and that the City Council now
became a Romanian institution. The Jew Armin Fein, not at all conver-
sant with the new official language, was suddenly an alderman no longer.
Retired all the way! Karl still managed to graduate from the Hungarian *Real Gymnasium* before it too became the Romanian *Liceu Constanin
Diaconovici Loga,* and was now headed for higher studies, but the cupboard
was bare. Armin summoned his firstborn and they sat down at the dining
table.

"Look, we cannot, I repeat cannot give you one penny for your studies. I
am sorry, it is certainly not the way I envisaged things, but I put everything
on the wrong horse. How was I to know that after all that fighting there
won't even be a Kaiser left? How?"

"But father, I don't need any money, I can make do on my own."

"That may be so, but we are two old people" Armin was fifty, Jozsa in
her thirties, "And there are certain duties the young have towards their
elders, sons towards their fathers. I have decided to go into retirement and
I expect you Karl to support your father and his wife, think of all the sacri-
fices they have made for your good."

"I am going to study, I want to become a doctor"

"Like Maxi?"

"No, a doctor who knows what he does and washes his hands before he
does it."

"So you want to make a lot of money and let your father and brothers
starve, what do you care?"

"No father, I'll send you some money."

"At the University it must be growing on trees, I presume"

"Why don't you ask your brother for help?"

"How *dare* you say that?"

"I'll send you a fixed amount each month, and when I come back I'll
support you all in style."

"If we are still alive"

"Don't be melodramatic father, please."

"Don't you ever speak to your own father like that. Apologize, this
instant!"

"All right, I apologize … I apologize.!"

At this point both father and son got up and left the dining room
through different doors. Armin headed for the bedroom, he felt tired and

needed a nap. Karl headed for the front door and rushed out to pay a visit
to his uncle Dr. Maxi Fein.

Karl got to his uncle's place just as Maxi and his wife were about to sit
down for lunch. The maid was serving the soup. In the dark dining room
the prevailing smell was not that of food but rather the heavy, smoky, dusty
smell of a place from which fresh air and sunlight have long been banished.
Maxi had ordered all windows shuttered up, lest nosy passers-by wise up to
what was going on inside. Since Aranka's death Maxi has had a few brushes
with disaster, but in the end things had worked out each time. Lunch was
the time of day when Maxi liked to be alone, or with his wife, which made
little difference. He met her when she started working for him many years
earlier as a nurse, and after marrying her, he treated her as a domestic. At
Karl's entrance the maid gave her master an inquisitive glance, as if asking whether she should add a setting, but the cool annoyed look on Maxi's
face made it clear that his nephew was not invited for lunch and in fact was
expected to state his business, get a reply, and be on his way, the quicker,
the better.

"Uncle Maxi," Karl started "I finished high school and I want to study
medicine"

"Don't you say so"

"My father cannot afford to send me to the University. That's all right,
I can manage, but my father has decided to go into retirement ..."

"I'm not surprised, the way he managed his affairs"

Karl ignored this remark, "You know he is wiped out financially, what
I would like to ask you ..."

"I knew sooner or later you're going to ask me for something. Well
young man, I am not even interested in listening to your request, if you
want to *schnorr*, go elsewhere, I am not a charitable institution. I work hard
for a living, and I watch my earnings carefully, no Imperial bonds for me"
at this Maxi started laughing with gusto, his whole face was shaking, the
big wart on his right cheek was executing an oscillatory motion.

Karl went on unperturbed, "All I want is to make you a proposition"

"Listen to this, a 'proposition' he calls it"

"As I told you I don't ask anything for me"

"Then why do you find it necessary to pester me at this hour and dis-
turb my peace?"

"What I am trying to say, if you'd but let me finish …while I am away at my studies I would like to ask you …"

"'Ask you', here you go again"

"Yes, ask you to give my father a reasonable monthly allowance and you have my word, I'll repay every last penny with interest as soon as I start earning money."

"And when would that be, may I ask?" Maxi threw a derisive look at Karl, then turned to his wife who started laughing, Maxi joined her in the laughter, while at the same time waving the maid out of the room, "So you want me to support your father after all he has done to me … are you crazy?"

"What has he done to you?"

"What? … Like I have to explain to you. He accused me of killing your mother …"

"Well, she died, didn't she?"

"Through no fault of mine"

"Oh let's not start all that blaming, that was a long time ago"

"He is not speaking to me to this day, and you, you little fart you, you think you can fool me? You blame me too. A doctor … some kind of doctor … *you* a doctor … now that's a laugh. You're just as dumb as my brother … a doctor indeed. I know just what I'll give you." Maxi turned to his wife "Fetch me that pair of pants I gave you to mend." The woman left and Maxi stared ahead, as if entirely alone "A doctor … some doctor". The woman returned carrying a pair of worn gray pants with a hole at the right knee.

"Take these," said Maxi "Don't mend the hole, it'll come in handy when you go begging … like my brother you are a *schnorrer* … a beggar … a doctor indeed … and now be gone!"

A startled Karl took the pants and left. A week later he was on the train for Kolozsvár to register at the University for the summer term. Youth has its own momentum and will always find a way, even among ruins.

KOLOMAN'S CROSS

God Almighty Himself, like many a soprano and tenor before Him, found out the hard way, Koloman Goldreich, the music critic of the *Temesvarer Tagesblatt*, was not easy to please. Jewish by birth, Koloman decided at the age of forty-three, a rather late stage as such things go, that the phrasing of the Old Testament, like that of many an aria he had to review, was not to his liking. One fine summer day in 1936 Koloman opted for the glories of Catholicism and with great fanfare had himself baptized by Archbishop Pacha, no less. He had brought his phonograph along to church and while the prelate was sprinkling him with fresh holy water, a celebrated recording of Schubert's *Ave Maria* was providing the right phrasing for the event. When they left the Kossuth Square Cathedral, Koloman's chest was sporting a golden cross rivaling in size that of His Eminence.

Henceforth Koloman would not be seen uncrossed. He wore his cross to the opera, he wore it to the concert hall, to the theater. He wore it even to the urinal, when attending a longer performance. Moreover, wherever he went, people could perceive him as radiating enthusiasm and deep feeling for his newly found Lord. This meant a lot to Koloman, for he wanted everyone to take his conversion for the principled act he had intended it to be and not for the opportunistic rear guard action his former coreligionists suspected.

He brought to his new religion a healthy dose of fanaticism. He could no longer overlook the superficiality and perfumed artificiality of Jewish composers. Mendelssohn, Meyerbeer and even Bizet came in for long and, in Koloman's mind, long-deserved criticism. In truth Koloman was not all that original, all these points, valid or not, had been made long before him by Wagner, but someone had to import them to the Banat and it fell on the freshly baptized Koloman Goldreich to be the agent of eugenics in the musical life of Temesvar, the Banatian capital. This was the right time for eugenics, for even in Beethoven's homeland a man's worth was established by the size of his foreskin. Should these criteria also be transplanted to the Banat, Koloman's cross could come in handy, as even the most callous SS-man would think twice before taking on a fellow sporting a ten centimeter cross of fourteen karat gold on his chest. Bishop Pacha of course knew that his new convert was one foreskin short and Bishop Pacha was a personal friend of the Führer. To Koloman's mind, this very fact established beyond the shadow of a doubt, his own good faith as far as his conversion was concerned.

Moral issues now weighed heavily on Koloman's thinking. This was reflected in his writing. He did not limit his pieces to critical evaluations of the music and its performance, but started digressing on the intrinsic moral and artistic limitations of Jewish composers. As one thing led to another, Koloman Goldreich came to the insight that these shortcomings were not specific to the arts, but that "the Jew" was incapable of a solid moral existence and as such acted as a corrupting agent in Western civilization. He penned article upon article exposing Jewish decadence and immorality. These articles were well received in a by then fascist Temesvar and even earned Bishop Pacha's praise.

It was at this point, in the spring of 1937 during a chance meeting on the Corso that Elemer Silberstein, Koloman's childhood friend, inadvertently blurted out to Koloman, that on the opening night of the opera season there was to be a big party in the nude at the Rosenthal villa. Koloman saw this as the ideal piece of evidence for his case against the corrupting influence of the Jew. Here on an occasion of highest cultural standing, when a star of the Vienna Staatsoper was to grace a new production of *Der Rosenkavalier*, what does the city's Jewish elite think of, but an opportunity to frolic in the nude and engage in God knows what unspeakable acts at the villa of a textile wholesaler whose only achievement in life amounted to having bought three wagons of cotton the year the Mississippi flooded and to have had luck in the way he invested his windfall. Koloman knew he had to attend. He could then break the story in his column and qualify, as it were, as an investigative reporter of some distinction. Unfortunately the party was by invitation only. Could Elemer Silberstein get him in somehow?

"You owe this to me, to your old friend."

"That would not be fair to the Rosenthals."

As it happened, Elemer Silberstein's wife Mitzi, the pianist, had a recital scheduled the night before the opera was to open and Koloman was to review it. So Koloman, with as much innocence as he could muster, asked Elemer "Isn't that just the night after Mitzi's recital?"

At this ominous question Elemer appeared at a loss for words, but after a brief struggle with his better self managed to make the suggestion Koloman expected of him

"You're right, we'll still be so tired, we won't be able to go anyway, so why don't you just take our invitation, let the Rosenthals say what they want."

"I am sure Mitzi's recital will be a great success, give her my love."

On this auspicious remark the two old friends parted and as agreed, in a couple of days Koloman received Elemer Silberstein's invitation to the Rosenthal soirée in the mail. The printed invitation did not specify the guest's name, so it could be used by the bearer.

From his orchestra seat at the *Rosenkavalier* premiere, Koloman eagerly surveyed the boxes with his opera glasses. There, to his eyes ostentatiously as always, sat the Rosenthals, the Grüns, the Wolfs and all the other Jews listening to the Marschallin bemoan the flow of time. The ladies in their Schiaparelli and Chanel dresses imported from Paris, were literally aglow in the sparkle of their diamonds and rubies. To think that all this fashion and all these adornments were to be shed, when after the undoing of the Baron Ochs, these ladies and their husbands in tails would repair to the secluded Rosenthal villa and act as if Sodom and Gomorrah had not made it into the Old Testament. But wait, just you wait!

After the end of the performance Koloman, still in tails, headed for his office to write his piece for the morning edition. From the notes he had jotted down during the performance a glowing review made it onto the page in less than an hour. By then, Koloman figured, the orgy would be in full swing and he could get the scoop of his career. After handing his review to the night-clerk, Koloman called a cab and headed for the Rosenthal mansion by the park.

He rang the bell at the wrought iron front door and was immediately admitted to the brightly lit red marble staircase leading up to the quite dark entrance hall. There, much to his surprise, Koloman was received by a maid whose one-piece uniform consisted of a well starched white bonnet on her head. Koloman wanted to proceed on through the door to the big hall, from which along with all the loud chatter and the noise of crystal, china and silverware, the sound of live music, probably produced by a naked Gypsy band, could be heard. With a disarming smile, the maid signaled to Koloman that he was expected to undress before gaining admission to the party. The maid then pointed towards a large pile of clothing, floor-length evening gowns, tails, shirts, top-hats, shoes and underwear, all thrown on top of each other in no particular order or system. When lust overcomes the Jew he loses all semblance of civilization, Koloman mused as he reluctantly started shedding his clothes and arranging them into a neat little pile at some distance from the revelers' garments . When in his briefs, he gave the maid a last imploring glance, but this rigorous admissions officer, politely raised her bare shoulders to signal that everything must come off before admission would be granted. Koloman was somewhat embarrassed. At 5'4" he did not have a physique that stands up well to scrutiny, not only was he completely bald, but his baldness had a polished sheen, his lean and far from muscular body was covered in sickly white skin and to see, he wore thick glasses. When totally naked, Koloman gave an uncertain inquisitive look in the maid's direction, and this, though indecently attired, still decent woman smiled encouragingly at Koloman, who headed for the sculptured door to the big hall. The maid quickly opened it and let Koloman in.

Coming from the dingy entrance hall, Koloman was blinded as he entered the well-lit premises. There in front of him stood the cream of Temesvar Jewry dressed to kill, the ladies' karats adding to the glare. As they all stared at Koloman, they saw a doubly well-hung oxymoronic apparition, for on his chest, a safe distance above his circumcised *schmuck*, a ten centimeter golden cross was also pointing towards the ground which refused to swallow him.

FEEDING THE PIRANHAS

When Willy Kardos told me about his idea, I thought he had lost his mind. Why on earth would two Jews, less than one year after the fall of Berlin, help high-ranking Nazis escape what they had coming to them? On the other hand the idea had a certain elegance, in its own way it contained an element of justice, even revenge. Anyway, if *we* weren't going to do it, some enterprising locals would willingly oblige, so what had we got to lose? In spite of my initial reservations, I came around and went along.

As for Willy, I fully trusted him, he and I go back a long way. With fake papers, we fled fascist Romania together. Like our deposed sovereign and his Jewish mistress we also ended up in neutral Portugal and sat the war out in a bearable internment camp. Between the two of us we had some money, not very much, but enough to get us through the bad times and then to get us started again quite comfortably after the war.

The morning after Willy laid out his plan at my two-room Lisbon apartment near the Cais do Sodré, yjr ywo of us were aimlessly milling on the pier, next to the building where one booked passage for South America. Munching crisp Portuguese potato chips to pass the time, we saw our first two customers leaving the building, carrying two leather suitcases each. One was a tall, tense blond mean-looking fellow, the other an older bald somewhat disoriented fat man wearing wire-frame glasses with thick lenses. They were conversing in German, sure that in this out-of-the-way place no one could possibly understand them. They were cursing the Portuguese travel agent who had refused to book them passage to Brazil for German

19

marks. Why should he? Those marks weren't worth the paper they were printed on, Germany had been defeated and its currency was worthless.

This was the moment we had been waiting for. I flashed a few hundred dollars at Willy and in the German dialect of the Romanian Banat, loudly suggested to him we go try our luck at the casino in Estoril. Just as we were leaving to catch the bus, the blond fellow mysteriously approached and in a whisper indicated that he couldn't help overhearing us and that he was immensely pleased at finally meeting fellow Germans with whom one could meaningfully talk for a change and not some more of these barbarian local crooks. Having noticed the wad of money in my hand, he proposed a deal. He would sell me his gold cigarette case for two passages to Rio. To sweeten the deal he proudly explained that he had served on the Eastern front and there, had personally been in charge of rounding up hundreds of Jews and ridding the earth of this vermin, "Now if they catch me, those stupid Americans, no telling what they would do with me. They wouldn't understand I just did my job, I did what had to be done by someone." At this he looked intently at me with an expression of 'you are German, you understand, it is your duty to help me'.

I took a look at his cigarette case. It was quite heavy and bore the inscription

> "Far
>
> > mein
> >
> > > Yankele
> > >
> > > > Deborah"

"Alas" I answered "I don't smoke and a used cigarette case would not fetch enough for me to even break even. But what else have you got in those suitcases?" This question made the blond German quite uncomfortable, and he evasively replied "Nothing of value." I made a gesture of 'sorry in that case I can be of no help' and Willy and I started walking away. Quite desperately the German called his friend and then motioned us to follow him. We walked for a good ten minutes until he found a secluded corner where we could continue in some privacy. The two Germans opened their luggage. The first suitcase was filled with large denomination mark bills. With a bitter smile they both conceded the worthlessness of all this cash. The remaining three suitcases, on the other hand, were filled with stock certificates issued by various German corporations, Daimler, Siemens, Telefunken, IG Farben, BMW, and many others. These were worthless as well, all they certified was the ownership of shares in a heap of rubble, for that is what Germany had been reduced to at that point. Willy took me aside to talk things over. After conferring for a short time, we returned to the Germans and Willy suggested that given the urgency of the situation and the services rendered by the two Germans to the Reich, we were willing to book passage to Rio for both of them against the three stock-filled suit-cases. It was a deal. After we purchased them passage, the Germans thanked us and took their leave by stretching their right arms in unrequited "Heil Hitler!" salutes, a weird gesture if you think of it, the Führer having com-mitted suicide months earlier. We let it pass.

This kind of transaction repeated itself with minor variations dozens of times over the following month. By the time scores of Nazis had gotten their passage to Rio, we were in possession of thirty leather suitcases each. The used leather suitcases themselves were worth about a quarter of what we had "invested" in the deals, but as to their contents that was an alto-gether different matter. For the time being it was worthless. Would it ever gain some value? At this point no one could tell, it was all a very risky speculation after all. Even storing the bulky stuff was far from trivial. My suitcases took up much of one of the two rooms of my small apartment. Time kept flowing and each year sprinkled another layer of white dust and black grime on my thirty pieces of luggage. The score was clearly Nazi Boys from Brazil thirty, Romanian Jews from Portugal love. But wait, just you wait till the Americans come to the rescue as they always do in the end. And did they ever, this time around!

The Americans came with their own plan, they called it the Marshall plan. The idea was to put Germany back on her feet and keep the Germans eating till they all became so fat, that they could no longer plot revenge, all they could do was take long naps to sleep off all those potatoes and all that beer. This much is well known. What is less well known, is the fine print of General Marshall's — what a bizarre name, if you think of it — plan. On one of the inside pages there is an innocuous little clause according to which all prewar stock certificates in surviving German corporations will have to be honored. It certainly does not say so in order to make sure that Nazis in Brazil should reap a windfall with stocks they stole from gassed Jews and which still remained in their possession even after they were fleeced on a Lisbon pier by a pair of Romanian Jews. It certainly does not say so in order to make sure that the Romanian Jews who purchased passage to

Brazil for said Nazis should reap a windfall either. Then why does it say so? That should not be hard to guess. Along with those gassed Jews, those fleeing Nazis and those Romanian Jews roaming the Lisbon piers, also some Americans, call them Rockefellers, Fords, Whitneys, whatever, also owned such shares and, unlike the gassed Jews, the fleeing Nazis, or the Romanian Jews, *they* had clout with the General, or should I say Marshall "you know George, why should only those krauts reap the benefits of the American taxpayer's generosity, while we lose our silk Sulka shirts? That wouldn't be fair, now, would it?"

Barely had the Marshall Plan been announced, than all of Lisbon fell prey to a German stock fever. These German stocks were rising so wildly, they were being likened to Dutch tulips. For me this was the moment to enter the room of the thirty suitcases. They were filthy, of course, so I asked Manuela the maid to give them a thorough dusting. For years she had been pestering me to throw them out, "They just take up room and collect dust" she would say. But I had some blind, and to be honest, unconscious faith in their value, I was sure their day would come sooner or later. Manuela removed three bucketfuls of dust and grime from the suitcase room and had opened the windows to air it out. It was a balmy spring evening, and the setting sun reflected by the river was enveloping the whole room in a golden glow. This was quite appropriate, for as I opened the first suitcase, out fell shares of Siemens, Bayer and DKW made out to bearer. It was clear, I was sitting on a goldmine. But what if these certificates could be traced?. I was Jewish, I had spent the war years in Portugal, I had the papers and the witnesses to prove it, so no one could accuse me of having gassed Jews in Auschwitz. Still, questions could be asked, and even if I was blameless, these shares could all be confiscated and my investment would go up in smoke.

I decided I had to look up Willy Kardos. We had lost touch since those days on the pier. We had never talked about what happened there, we just started scrupulously avoiding each other. We had done nothing illegal, we both knew that much, but the suitcases, some of fine croc, of black suede, of patent leather, of nubuck, were reeking of Jewish blood and we both knew that as well. I could bear the stench of my own suitcases, but not that of Willy's. I wouldn't be surprised to learn that Willy felt the same way. Now we couldn't avoid it, we had to talk. It was clear that first these stocks had to be thoroughly laundered. Willy had a different problem as well, he had gotten married to Ada, a classy Jewish woman from Budapest and Ada had opened some of his suitcases and decorated the living room walls in German stocks. She might as well have used gold leaf. The shares could not be peeled off the wall. Still Willy and I had a good fifty suitcases between the two of us and even after their recent dusting they were all in bad need of laundering. We had to find a place with a proper appreciation of the virtues of both cleanliness and discretion. Almost in unison we shouted out "Switzerland" and for all I know, we may thereby have invented the art of asset laundering.

So, off to Zurich we traipsed Willy, Ada and I. With six of our suitcases we appeared at a private bank on that city's famed Bahnhoffstrasse. We were obviously not the first post-Marshall arrivals at this financial institution, for the officer who attended to our business knew full well what we were after. Had this Swiss banker invented asset laundering before us? Well, who ever gets credit for that invention, we got title to our stocks. It was a complicated transaction channeled through Liechtenstein and Geneva, and to a certain extent, I am convinced, through this officer's pocket. I don't know whether to this day I fully understand the intricacies of this process. Be that as it may, we counted out the various shares all made out to bearer and one month later got shares registered in our names as of April 1st 1937. The chosen date added a touch of irony, maybe the officer or one of his superiors had a reaped a windfall of their own. After all, we only got seventy registered shares for every hundred bearer-shares we sent to be laundered. But there was plenty to go around and seventy percent of a fortune is still very much a fortune.

For the next two months we were commuting between Lisbon and Zurich and by summer we were millionaires. Now we could go to Estoril, not to the slot machines as before, but to the rooms where old ladies play canasta. We once landed in a game with our former sovereign's Jewish former mistress and by now wife, Her Highness the Duchess Elena Magda Lupescu. She was very moved at our fluency in the Romanian language, sprinkled as it was with Yiddish words all over. Each time we used one of these words, she would wink at us as befits a blue-blooded Jewish Duchess.

It was not all roses from here on. With half his money, Willy bought himself a diamond mine in Angola. He did so over Ada's objections, who then absconded with the other half. That fool had given her signature rights to his Swiss account. But, between us, even all by itself, an Angolan diamond mine still made for a very, very comfortable livelihood in Salazar's Portugal. I was more conservative and had no Hungarian or any other kind of better half. Yet, Willy's diamonds scintillating under the strong African sun, just as my assets on the books of a Swiss bank were still redolent with the stench of ovens where Jews were burned. It took me years to come to terms with this inescapable fact of life. But before I reached that point of serenity, I paid for those tickets to Rio with thick lines on my forehead and with the severe pain in my chest called forth by my guilty Jewish heart. Willy paid even more dearly. Beware when the Gods reward you in cash. Beware!

It all started with Ada. I am not trying to blame her, but if there is an event which started the ball rolling, her trip to Zurich was it. Ostensibly she left to talk to our Swiss attorney — you cannot launder assets without an attorney — and take care of some odds and ends, which needed taking care of, before the matter of Willy's finances could be considered as having been fully legitimized. On our previous trips to Zurich, it was Willy and I who were dealing with the attorney, a corpulent fiftyish gentleman, as honorable and perfectly on the up and up, as one could expect in a matter like asset laundering. To keep Ada taken care of, the attorney offered the services of his assistant, a tense and frustrated, good-looking young man. This arrangement would rightfully have triggered Willy's jealous watchfulness, were it not for the fact that this young man was the attorney's live-in lover, as they both openly admitted with a naughty smile. While Willy and I were being initiated into the legal fine points of the labyrinthine scheme of transactions intended to cleanse the contents of our suitcases, this young assistant was escorting Ada through the elegant boutiques, movie houses and theatres of this bourgeois haven not ravaged by war and it was all so safe, for this young man had openly registered his partiality to members of his own sex, which according to our Romanian-Portuguese-Jewish background clearly implied a total lack of interest on his part in members of the opposite sex in general and therefore in Ada in particular. Little did we suspect that in the city of Carl Gustav Jung a man's sexual preferences were far from binding and could be switched at a moment's notice, especially during an episode of asset laundering. When Ada returned to make the final arrangements, she was picked up at the railway station by the young assistant, and they proceeded directly to the bank, where Ada transferred the balance of Willy's account into a new account the assistant had opened in her name. The assistant then followed up by initiating divorce proceedings on Ada's behalf and at least in spirit, if not in quite in fact, given the circumstances, Ada became betrothed to the young man. As Ada had no further financial demands on her spouse, the divorce was expeditiously granted and the attorney's lover wed his client's ex-wife in a — by local standards — ethically proper ceremony.

Willy was despondent. Like most suddenly wised-up husbands, he could only comprehend his predicament in terms of a conspiracy. The villain was clearly the Swiss attorney who lusting after Willy's money, had treated him to the charade of his assistant-lover, "No one can do it both with men and women, either you are this or you are that, that's obvious, isn't it?" was the way he put it.

Against my better judgment I tried to explain to my friend and former business partner that the way things happen in the real world was much more complex and that such ambiguous sexual preferences were not unheard of even in a country in which the sidewalks were regularly scrubbed clean with soap and hot water in the interest of public hygiene. Willy could not and would not even contemplate this possibility. The way he coped with my raising it, was by suitably extending the scope of the conspiracy and including me among the conspirators. He accused me of having been Ada's lover and in the end swore never again to speak to me, "You filthy Nazi" that's what he called me. Unlike Ada, the Swiss attorney and the Swiss attorney's assistant, I was at hand and within weeks after this parting of ways Willy started suing me in the local Portuguese courts for everything conceivable: alienation of affections, adultery, fraud, black-marketeering. He had no chance of winning, but he had a good go at making my life miserable and wasting my money on legal fees.

Willy showed up in court with a notorious Lisbon ambulance chaser, one Luis Barroso de Castro, a fat old totally asexual creature with a wino's nose. His assistant, most certainly *not* his lover, a soft-spoken black-haired dark fellow with long dirty fingernails approached my attorney with the proposition that against a substantial remuneration, Luis Barroso de Castro was willing to commit an error which would get the case thrown out by the judge. It would have been an easy way to end the matter, but it would have literally made me join an anti-Willy conspiracy and I just couldn't bring myself to do that.

With all the shenanigans of the ever-increasing ranks of Lisbon attorneys involved in it, this matter kept dragging on for years. It finally was going to come to a head in a hearing in front of a senior judge. Just as Luis Barroso de Castro was in the process of wrapping up his three-hour introductory oration, Willy's maid showed up and handed Willy a letter. By its appearance it must have arrived from abroad by express mail. I watched Willy nervously fumble with it until he finally succeeded in ripping it open and started reading it. A few pages into this letter, tears started forming in Willy's eyes and his hands started shaking as if suddenly he had been afflicted with Parkinson's disease. He valiantly read on, and just as his attorney was raising his gravelly voice to emphasize the injuries allegedly inflicted by me on his client, Willy collapsed. Everybody rushed to his side, but to no avail. Willy had succumbed to an irreversible infarct.

Even the loquacious Barroso de Castro was at a loss for words. But he, the judge and just about everyone else in the courtroom was curious to know what could possibly have been in the letter that had such a fatal impact on its addressee. Though on shaky legal ground, yet without any protests from any of the many attorneys present, the judge ordered the letter to be handed to him. He looked at it page by page and then announced that it was written in code. Through my attorney I asked the judge's permission to inspect the letter. Permission was granted, probably on the basis of the judge's own curiosity. It turned out that the code used by the writer was the Hungarian language.

The letter was from Ada. Starting with its first line it had an extremely apologetic tone. Apparently, one year after marrying her, the young assistant dropped her for a handsome young Zurich man, also an attorney. He was still a legal assistant, but the handsome young attorney was now his boss for a change. Ada's second divorce had been painful and the professional legal assistant had walked away with half her share of Willy's expensively laundered assets. The handsome young attorney had been around all along it turned out, and the legal assistant's marriage to the Hungarian lady had been a sham. Its only goal had been the acquisition of a nest egg for the young Swiss lovers. Now, more than a year after this divorce, the lady started feeling the pangs of guilt. She'd been had the same way Willy had been. Though she wanted a secure existence for herself, she felt that she

had kept too much of Willy's money, and on the very page Willy was reading when his heart gave out, she offered to voluntarily surrender to Willy
the bulk of her remaining assets.

With the plaintiff gone, the case was dismissed, much to the regret
of the assembled attorneys. I went back to my new home, a sumptuous
eighteenth century *palacio*, which I had bought for a pittance. I sat down
on the big chair in the hanging garden overlooking the Tagus. It was cool.
I enjoyed the fountain's murmur. I fell asleep. I saw seven large canoes
manned by Amazonian aborigines being swiftly rowed down the Tagus. A
gasmask wearing Nazi officer, cracking a long whip was seated at the head
of each canoe. When they got near the pier, the officers jumped off and
swam as best they could towards an anchored ship. The aborigines jumped
helter-skelter off their un-coxed canoes as well, but without gasmask pro-
tection they stood no chance, they were instantly devoured by the agitated
gasmask wearing piranhas indigenous to the river. The empty canoes were
freely floating toward the shore. Their cargo of electric motors, cars, radio
sets and overripe Limburger cheese was being unloaded by two Lubavich-
ers in their black caftans and broad-brimmed felt hats into a truck painted
with the Romanian tricolor. For every two unloaded items one was thrown
in the water to appease the hungry piranhas. The fully loaded truck took
off for an unknown destination in the Sierra. As the road climbed steeply,
the Lubavicher driver started shrinking away until he totally disappeared,
leaving the truck in free roll. It was precisely at this moment that the other
Lubavicher, after having crossed himself both in the Eastern and in the
Catholic manner, took over and stopped the truck. He opened the back
hatch. The stench of the Limburger was overwhelming. The Lubavicher,
holding his nose, climbed on the truck and was about to scatter its contents
to the winds, when suddenly he took a deep breath and a satisfied smile,
extending from one ear-lock to the other settled on his long beard as he
uttered the words "Ah, that perfume, I love it."

MALICIOUS INTENT

Momentous decisions can rarely be traced to specific instants in time. Even where this seems possible, careful consideration will reveal a latent germination period. Still, Jiři Weissmann would forcefully insist that his mind was made up suddenly, as if by illumination, when on a lazy Sunday afternoon in Skokie his American host asked him "and you didn't raise a stink?" Jiři had been going over what he liked to call his Monte Cristo experience. and suddenly the method that would exact both vengeance and justice — they had gotten hopelessly enmeshed in his mind — revealed itself to him.

Like Dumas' Count, Jiři had met his own potential benefactor while in detention, though not on a forbidding Mediterranean rock, but in Dachau, just outside Munich. The Funks, father and son were killed there in 1944, one year before the end. "Mr. Weissmann, you know, in Pressburg we were very rich" old Mr. Funk had said. Jiři knew, he had often shopped at the Funk department store in the city center and it was common knowledge in Pressburg, that half an hour's tram-ride away you could shop at Funk's elegant Vienna branch on the Mariahilferstrasse. "Well Mr. Weissmann" the emaciated old man went on "we are not going to get out of this alive. My boy, he has TB, and our turn is coming soon anyway. I want you to know, I have five million American dollars at the Schweizer Sozialbank in Zurich on the Bahnhoffstrasse. It's all in a numbered account 12111879 — that's my dear wife's birth date, she died on the way here. We tried to get to Zurich, but they turned us back at the border. If you ever get out of here, I *want* you to claim that money. I don't want those ganefs to keep it. You can

29

rightfully tell them, I gave it to you, you'll know the number, what more can those damn bastards want?"

As feared, the last of the Funks met their end one week to the day after this revelation. Jiři, well, he had a strong physique and made it out of Dachau. Shortly after being freed, he took off for the Bahnhoffstrasse, only to be politely turned back at the border "But Mr. Weissmann, the war is over now and you have nothing to fear. Without a valid visa we cannot admit you to Switzerland".

A Swiss visa was not hard to come by in occupied Vienna, like everything else it had a price, not a particularly stiff one at that. Ten days later Jiři was back and this time he successfully entered Switzerland as soon as he paid 4.52 francs customs on his pipe tobacco and on some other items found on him by the methodical Swiss customs agent. At the Sozialbank he was received by one Kurt Frauenfelder, a well-fed and well- groomed dark skinned fellow with large teeth and a sharp aquiline nose, whose looks could have qualified him for anything between a two-legged horse and a greedy bird of prey. In a small office looking out on a dark courtyard, Herr Frauenfelder heard out the freshly released Jew, all the while nervously tapping with his smartly manicured fingers the walnut table which separated them. Rather mechanically he then embarked on a speech of his own. It argued that short of a proof of death and of a properly notarized document to support his claim, there could be no further meaningful discussion on this matter. Herr Frauenfelder could not even confirm the existence of the Funk account at the Sozialbank, for that would violate Swiss banking secrecy laws. For Jiři's benefit he concluded on a moralistic note "Look Herr Weissmann, we in Switzerland are aware of the somewhat unfortunate and not quite fair treatment of your co-religionists by the Third Reich and I can understand your distress following a lengthy detention under unusual circumstances." He punctuated this subdued expression of empathy by raising his upper lip and baring his front-teeth in what he was sure would pass for a smile. "But now all this is over and if I may give you a piece of advice, get on with your life. Forget such get-rich-quick schemes. Good day to you and be sure to let me know if I can be of any service to you in the future, on some other matter."

At that point in his life what Jiři needed above all was peace, so, one windfall the poorer, he settled in sunny Nice, where he opened a restaurant. Things worked out and he put Dachau successfully behind him. He got married and led a sheltered existence for a change.

It was not until 1962 that the Funk fortune reappeared in Jiři's life. According to the newspapers, the State of Israel was claiming the funds in inactive prewar accounts of presumably massacred Jews. Trouble was, honoring such a claim would have involved a systematic search of the books of all Swiss banks, which was inadmissible, as it violated those same secrecy regulations. The Israelis were willing to settle for a "one-man-commission" to inspect the books, the "one man" being none other than the president of the Swiss Confederation. This was still unacceptable to the Swiss, there was a principle to uphold and this principle was sacrosanct. It was certainly not going to be overturned for a claim of "a very few million dollars". To settle the matter, the Swiss banks offered to "donate" one million to the young Levantine nation against her dropping the claim. It was a take-it-or-leave-it deal that was supposedly taken. The press labeled the Swiss banks "the vultures of Europe". This all died down soon, but in Jiři an anger, a fury of vast proportions was kindled. Dachau was behind him now, but Zurich's famed Bahnhoffstrasse lay there prospering on Jewish blood. Why were the Jews turned back at the border in the Thirties? "Grandmother, why do you have such strict secrecy in banking laws?" Jiři found himself asking in his ever more frequent retelling of the Funk business. A form of impotent rage entered his story where it lay smoldering for over a decade until that fateful Skokie afternoon.

Upon his return from America, Jiři took off right away on a three week Swiss vacation with his wife Renée. A plan had been hatched and was now to be executed. In Zurich a conservatively dressed Jiři, sporting a black leather attaché case, showed up at the Sozialbank. He asked for and was introduced to Herr Kurt Frauenfelder, now completely bald and paralyzed on the right half of his face, probably as the result of a stroke ... oh all that Swiss cheese! He did not recognize Jiři, which was just as well, for he now introduced himself as Georges Dreyfuss, a French attorney, and upon request produced an appropriate fake ID. He wanted to rent a safe. Frauenfelder found this a smart move for a Frenchman, given the Swiss secrecy in banking.

With the formalities out of the way, Jiři was shown to a private cabin where he proceeded to transfer the contents of his attaché case into the safe box. One by one he unloaded into the box seven packages of Limburger cheese in an early stage of fermentation, making sure all the wrappings were punctured. He closed the box, stayed a few more minutes, refreshed himself with cologne then called the attendant and locked the box in the vault. He made sure to thank Frauenfelder for his professional attitude and understanding.

A week of Gstaad skiing was thoroughly enjoyed by the French couple. Back in Zurich they registered at the staid Baur au Lac, whence Renée walked unaccompanied to the Sozialbank a few blocks away to open *her* safe for a change. She did not ask for M. Frauenfelder and identified herself as Christiane Dorléac. In the vault a penetrating odor not unlike that of sweaty feet could not go unnoticed. Renée asked whether there was another vault. Much to the regret of the bank officer, this was the only vault the bank kept. It was unusually large and fortified against a nuclear attack, much safer the officer volunteered than many weaker vaults vulnerable to such attack. "But it stinks in here, can't you tell?" Renée exclaimed with an expression of disgust that comes so naturally to speakers of the French language. A vaulted Arab nodded his agreement. The distraught officer offered Renée a perfumed towelette and a piece of rock candy, such as is routinely handed out on airplanes when turbulence sets in. "A sickness bag would be more appropriate" the lady sneered back, again meeting the wealthy Arab's approval. A Spaniard just locking his box joined in at this point "in the worst slums of Barcelona you do not get a stench this bad, but then, unlike you, we learned cleanliness from the Arabs. Maybe you should ask some of your Arab customers for hygienic advice". The officer was speechless. Renée returned to an ever-stronger stench for the next three days, but then on the fourth day the stench was gone, the bank had finally done something about it. Renée expressed her gratitude to the visibly proud officer. "You know the riffraff we get these days" his subservient smile seemed to suggest.

The Weissmanns returned to Nice and it took Jiři another month before he showed up at the Sozialbank in the company of a Zurich attorney. Led to his box, his key did not fit, but before he could register the expected amazement, as if on a signal, a battery of bank officers descended on him. In a tense whisper they invited Maître Dreyfuss to vice-president Frauenfelder's office. Jiři and his lawyer were seated on rigid brown leather armchairs, two officers behind each of them just in case they had their mind set on a nuclear attack or something. The visibly annoyed semi-paralyzed vice-president embarked, at quite some effort, on his speech. It started with a list of items most commonly stored in Sozialbank vaults, such as securities, jewelry, gold, cash, and emphasized the hygienic feasibility of their storage, no matter what their origin. He then came to his point "Maître Dreyfuss, there are certain items not fit for storage in a non-refrigerated vault. They cause an unhygienic environment and endanger public health. *Even* in France you must be aware of this, and we are all the more appalled at your callous disregard of our health regulations."

"Is there a law forbidding the storage of cheese in Swiss vaults?" Jiři interrupted.

"Not really, just plain common sense, Sir. I am sorry to say we had to force open your box, discard its decomposed contents and then rekey the box. Therefore at this time we charge you SF 523.42 for the damage and inform you that your vault privileges have been revoked."

"Wait, Herr Frauenzimmer."

"Frauenfelder, Maître" interjected the semi-paralyzed vice-president with a half-smile.

"Herr Frauenfelder then, are there no secrecy in banking laws on the books in Switzerland any longer?" At this Jiři and his attorney huddled to confer. Frauenfelder, sweating profusely on both the mobile and frozen halves of his face, responded, not without some hesitation "Of course there are, but they have to be suspended where public hygiene is at issue. Anyway, your 'perfumed' possessions have been discarded in the presence of representatives of the cantonal police. You can rest assured that no one ate your cheese"

"So you lifted banking secrecy for the sake of good odor and you discarded my valuables without even notifying me"

"You must appreciate our position. Were we to have notified you of the fate of your 'valuables', we may have risked never seeing you again and thus forfeiting the compensation due us for the damage and disturbance you caused."

"Come on now, do you know what that Limburger was wrapped in?"

"Paper and tinfoil, of course"

"Yes, and the paper had the legal proof of my claim to an account at your bank, the Funk account, number 12111879. You have violated banking secrecy on account of an odor which you perceived as offensive and you have robbed me of a fortune at the same time. The gentleman with me, a local colleague, assures me your actions are felonious under Swiss law. Therefore I demand that you open to me the Funk account without delay.

Otherwise I will be forced to take my case to the courts and the media. To me, Herr Frauenfelder, the stench of Jewish blood is even more offensive than that of German or Swiss cheese."

Frauenfelder was staring intently at Jiři, a glimmer of recognition hit the active half of his dark face, his lips nervously parted, revealing the yellow teeth, then his whole body jerked, the vice-president of the Schweizer Sozialbank experienced a second and this time fatal stroke.

"Now look what you have done" one of the standing bank officers exclaimed, as the boss's death became evident even to this man with an Appenzell accent.

"Are you accusing me of murder?" Jiři shouted back. The Swiss attorney warned "that is slander'"

"No, I apologize, I didn't mean it that way."

The rest went smoothly. Of course the Funk millions did not earn interest, since the owners had failed to re-negotiate the investment of their capital as of 1935, leading the bank to the natural assumption that they did not wish to collect interest on it.

DACHAU IDYLL

Lately I have been overcome by an urge to put my affairs in order, the end must be near. I can't complain though. My health seems to hold up, I have a cozy apartment overlooking solid red-roofed Bavarian houses and I enjoy the friendliness and respect of the good people of Dachau. Yes, I can say it in good conscience, I have achieved happiness in this lovely town. My Gabriel, may he rest in peace, is buried in the Catholic cemetery here and a place next to him is reserved for me and paid up for twenty-five years. For now I tend the grave, I quite enjoy doing so, it is so peaceful there and you meet nice people in the cemetery. When I am gone, my son will have to take care of it, he owes us that much, "the good Jew."

He rarely comes to visit, though we asked so little of him over the years. We ultimately accepted his remaining Jewish, though Gabriel had repeatedly tried to convince him and that Protestant wife of his to make a compromise and convert to Catholicism, the best religion by far. No, he had that shiksah convert to Judaism just to spite us, or as he likes to put it, to bring the children up Jewish, of all things. Once when we brought up the subject of his Jewishness, he suggested we all spend a vacation away from the monotony of Dachau, "say in Auschwitz?" He never understood us, we couldn't *afford* staying Jewish.

When we finally managed to get out of communist Romania in '59, according to the emigration papers we were supposed to be headed for Israel. But we weren't born yesterday, we didn't leave one hell to move to another. Yes, right away they would have taken my son to the military and

35

that clumsy boy, he would have fallen in some battle or other and then my Gabriel and I would have been left alone with no one to look after us in old age. So, Paris it was for us. My son got himself a fellowship and received his doctorate there, but *we* couldn't stay. We supported ourselves by selling a few of the diamonds we managed to get out, don't ask me how, yes, if you have to know, by hiding them *there*. But it couldn't go on like that for long, Gabriel and I had to do something.

Gabriel was a fine gynecologist, but with a prewar Berlin diploma they wouldn't let him practice in Paris, or anywhere else in Europe, outside of Germany. Sure, he could have taken an equivalence exam, the *nostrification* as they call it, but that would have been stupid. That exam is not meant to find out whether you qualify to practice with a foreign diploma, but to find something you don't know, the name of the nerve that runs from here to there, or some other nonsense like that, so they can keep the foreign competition out. The only hope we had, was to go to Germany and open a practice there. But you try and hang out your shingle in Germany as a Jew, even after Hitler. You think those Germans would allow a Jew to cut them up or bring them into this world? No way! Yes, they'd let a Jew drill their teeth or they'd even take little Helmut to a Jew if he runs a fever, but the Jew better keep his distance from the main battlefield of the war between the sexes. That's off limits for the Jew. *Strengstens verboten!*

When we showed up in Bonn with the request to settle there and ultimately to open a practice, a serious bespectacled official made it clear to us that while Gabriel's diploma was impeccable, to settle as foreigners was far from trivial. The only ones for whom settlement was automatic were *Auslandsdeutsche,* Germans from abroad. Dejectedly we left his office and took a train to shabbily rebuilt Cologne to see its famed cathedral. We were standing in front of that gray stone giant, watching the swift flow of the muddy Rhine when Gabriel came up with the remedy to our predicament. As he looked at a wooden horse swaying in the brisk wind, its poster announcing a vocal recital of songs on Heine texts, Gabriel exclaimed "that's it! we'll say we're German, we're *Auslandsdeutsche."*

We decided to continue on as far as possible from the bespectacled official and more or less at random settled on Munich. The only rational explanation I have for this choice is that both Gabriel and I were born in the Habsburg Empire and Bavaria was the closest you could get to that in Germany. To introduce ourselves as *Auslandsdeutsche* was not all that difficult, Gabriel had always been a Teuton at heart. He walked with determination, his speech was heavily cadenced, he carefully avoided any Levantine mannerisms: when speaking, he never used his hands, he never let his feet create the tell-tale Chaplinesque obtuse angle, he felt insulted if anyone took him for a Jew. His ideal was Erich von Stroheim, the quintessential German field marshal of the silver screen. We saw *Five Graves to Cairo* seven times at the very least. While I rooted for poor Anne Baxter and her Franchot Tone, Gabriel was winning the war for the Führer with Stroheim's General Field Marshal Erwin Rommel "We shall take that big fat cigar out of Mr. Churchill's mouth and make him say Heil." Come to think of it, our son, he couldn't tolerate even this minor hobby of Gabriel and in a wanton act of cruelty had to tell his father that Stroheim's accent in English was Viennese not Prussian and that Stroheim was a Jew. Von Stroheim a Jew! Whom was he kidding? You can explain Gabriel to his very last toe, if you think of him as a perpetually self-perfecting copy of Erich von Stroheim, Prussian officer, not Viennese Jew. My Gabriel knew better.

So, we made an appointment at the Bavarian resettlement office and with Prussian punctuality we showed up for it. To parade as *Auslandsdeutsche* with emigration papers made out for the Land of the Jews was far from easy, but we were prepared for the obstacles. We came from the Romanian Banat where a sizable Swabian population was known to reside. We both spoke fluent German and identified as Germans. The small detail that we were both born Jewish was incidental and we had tried to emigrate to Israel simply because that was the only emigration destination acceptable to the Romanian authorities. But we have never had the slightest intention of going to a country with which we felt no affinity, we were German through and through.

"How about religion?" Our answer to this question: we had converted to Catholicism long ago, before the war. Any proof? Hardly, after all we were coming out of a dictatorship like Romania headed for Israel. But we were well prepared for this question and named a former Swabian patient of Gabriel, one Anneliese Hund, who could swear to the fact that we were Catholics. Anneliese was a tall obese spinster, who had entrusted Gabriel with the medical maintenance of her chronic virginity. Anneliese badly needed a man in her life, but there being no mortal takers, had settled on her Lord as a spiritual substitute. This pious virgin was deeply disturbed to have her body tended to by a man who believed in only one component of the Trinity, so she made it her mission to make Gabriel accept the remaining two. In a blatant manner she started proselytizing for her Lord. Now she would give Gabriel a leather-bound copy of the New Testament, now a copy of both Testaments bound in one volume, now a rosary. After a while Gabriel, by nature not a religious man, got fed up with all this. To keep his patient happy, he swore her to secrecy and then told Anneliese that convinced by her arguments and without anyone knowing it, he and I had converted to Catholicism. This made Anneliese immensely happy and she gave Gabriel a gold-plated crucifix with the Savior's pain-contorted silver-plated body soldered to it. Given the strict prohibition against the exportation of precious metals from Communist countries, Gabriel couldn't possibly be expected to have brought out this cherished sacred object, which unlike compact diamonds, is not easily hidden in the human body. On the other hand Anneliese herself had left Romania for Germany right after the war and with a small effort should be traceable.

This story so moved the Bavarian official that he promised to locate Anneliese as fast as he could. He found her in less than a month and got from her an affidavit in which Anneliese confirmed all the details of our story, while at the same time taking ample credit for her missionary work. This way in early 1961 we both obtained German working permits. Given the remarkable spirituality of our past, the Bavarian official, a deeply religious man himself, saw to it that Gabriel found a job and let us know that as *Auslandsdeutsche,* one year after our arrival we will be entitled to a large sum of money from the government, should Gabriel wish to open a private practice then.

The task at hand was to choose a hospital at which to spend that first year. The official had given us a list of Bavarian hospitals with gynecology openings. There were fourteen listings, near Passau, near Würzburg, and in other distant places. There was nothing in Munich proper, but there were two listings in the Munich suburb of Dachau. At first we dismissed this tainted town as no place for two Jews, no matter how *Auslandsdeutsch* their credentials. Then it occurred to us that Dachau was the safest place for such Jews, for precisely in this setting, absolutely no one would dare start a serious investigation of their religious history. I felt ill at ease about this whole *Auslandsdeutsch* business at the time, but I understood that we had to make a living and that we weren't the youngest any longer. So, if a modest deception was what it took, so be it. No one would be the wiser. Anneliese Hund could be counted on, she was so proud of her missionary record.

The only fly in the ointment was my son. I therefore undertook a brief journey to Paris. The easiest thing would have been for him to join our mock-conversion, Anneliese could easily be induced to vouch for him as well. Yet, this obstinate boy would have none of it, the most I could make him promise was that if asked, he would confirm *our* Catholicism. Gabriel was very worried about the reliability of this promise, the young are not known to be all that careful. To safeguard our position then, we found it expedient to curtail our relations with our son. We certainly did not attend his Jewish wedding. For this my son blames me to this day, as if it were my fault. But honestly, he has no one to blame but himself, all we were asking of him was to *pretend* to be a Catholic, not to actually convert. If his parents weren't deserving of this minuscule sacrifice, then I must wonder whether I succeeded in rearing him properly, of impressing upon him the immense debt owed by each and every one of us to our parents.

Our arrival in Dachau was very well received, understandably so. Because of the town's stigma, they had not been able to get a gynecologist to accept a position there. The townspeople resented this very much. To deliver their children, the women of Dachau had to journey to Munich, to some big impersonal hospital, the act of giving birth was robbed of its traditional homey warmth. Sure, during the war some atrocities were committed in Dachau, but by the SS, not by the townspeople, same as elsewhere. So, say some Jews lost their lives there as claimed. Does this condemn the Dachau citizenry in perpetuity to a deprivation of the most basic services? Viewed from here, it appears as if the Jews were unfairly singling out idyllic Dachau for their habitual cruel vengeance.

In this atmosphere a Catholic shingle was of essence and we could provide one. That first year Gabriel started an Ob/Gyn section at the municipal hospital and local women came in droves to have their babies delivered there. This augured well for us, for in the second year when we would open the private practice, Gabriel would have a large population of satisfied patients to draw on. They all were very grateful to him.

Still, this was all predicated on our impeccable Catholic credentials. We had a local woman clean our place and even this good woman might notice that there was not a trace of Catholic life in our apartment. Something had to be done about that. At a fair in a nearby village I bought the portrait of a haloed woman piously looking heavenward, whence a bright white light shone upon her blue dress. According to local tradition this was unmistakably a portrait of the Blessed Virgin. Once hung over my bed this portrait would serve as a daily reminder to our cleaning woman that she was cleaning good Catholic dirt and not the reviled Jewish kind. At the same fair I also picked up a brass ashtray in the middle of which rose a cross to which was nailed the figure of a handsome Germanic youth rendered decent by a small loincloth. I placed this contraption on our coffee table and henceforth no one could smoke a Camel in our living room, without inhaling a trace of good Catholic spirituality. Beyond its practicality for the nicotine-addict, this sacred-looking object had the advantage that in a pinch, say a sudden visit from our son, it could quickly be hidden and then returned to its central location once the boy was gone. With this ashtray lording over our coffee table and the haloed woman's portrait over my bed, our reputation as a God-fearing pious couple was forcefully established, even against our dismal record of Holy Mass attendance.

There was another ingredient to our bogus pedigree, we couldn't cultivate any genuine friendships. After all, the hallmark of a genuine friendship is the ability to let one's defenses down and bare one's vulnerabilities. This was the one thing *we* could not afford. We had to stay alert at all times. Now, not making close friendships with Dachauers may not be such a great sacrifice. Yet, we all need others to stay in touch with, we need to relate, ever so superficially, to *someone*. We found an excellent medium for cultivating such relationships, we took up the game of bridge. We played as a team, us against them. Our conversation was highly formalized, bidding and pleasantries. Our actions were quite ritualized: shuffle, deal, eat, drink. And yet, even this rigid form of human relationship met our needs, we were not alone, much more even, we were accepted.

What was all this for? For this: without the hundred thousand marks we got from the German government, we would never have been capable of opening a practice, we could not even have played bridge, maybe Chinese checkers after mowing lawns all day. But without being *Auslandsdeutsche,* not a pfennig would have come our way from the German government. Finally, who has ever seen a pair of *Jewish Auslandsdeutsche?* So we decided to live the Catholic life, no Torah, no fasting at Yom Kippur, no tallis, no phylacteries, bareheaded before the Almighty, no more circumcisions either, unlike Romania, where many of Gabriel's patients had been Jewish. For sure no circumcisions!

Dachau is not in America where they circumcise even the Goyim. If you ask me why they do that, I'll have to reply like Frau Keller, our neighbor, that unlike our German variety, most American obstetricians are Jewish and that these Jewish doctors want to make sure that no one will ever be able to tell the Jew by his schmuck. Understandable, but hardly very different from what we did, if you think of it. Incidentally, Frau Keller came to this insight on a vacation in the Rockies, where she swallowed more than one of these circumcised American organs — her specialty, to believe the gossips, — and afterwards needed to make sure she hadn't whored for the Jew.

So, instead of all the Jewish paraphernalia, we have haloed portraits and crucified loin-clothed hunks, not so different after all. I really don't see what the fuss is all about, and there is fuss, just ask my son. But leave *me* in peace, I've heard it all, and it all sounds like a lot of baloney to me. If it all matters so much to him that's his problem, I have no doubt we did the right thing.

There was one close call though. Some years ago, around Christmas we were invited for a game at the house of our bridge club president. He had three tables going, twelve of us plus two alternate players. It was a major event in the president's dream villa away from the bustle of the city, in a rural part of town overlooking the former concentration camps. If you are not aware of what ever went on there, or if after all these years you are willing to suspend your awareness of it, it is really quite bucolic, idyllic. We watched the sunset and sipped Mosel before sitting down at the three tables. With the holidays around the corner, people were more outgoing, they were outright restless. A couple of hours into the game our hostess, plump Mathilde with auburn braids rolled around her rotund head, asked us to help ourselves to a, by Dachau standards, lavish buffet dinner: beef stew with hunter's sauce and dumplings and *sekt*, the German bubbly which is to French Champagne what a French Citroën Deux Chevaux is to a German Porsche. This may not sound like great food or great drink to former Habsburg subjects, but the elegance of the service made up for the culinary and enological shortcomings.

Be that as it may, people got very carried away, especially by the *sekt*. No one had expected such extravagance, coffee and cookies and some sandwiches was all that most of us had in mind. With all that booze, people lost interest in the game and for a change started talking like old friends. Of course, we had been playing together for years and had occasionally gossiped with each player about each other player. Still, now for a change we were all together and for a first time we could all relate to each other and thereby create a cohesive group with a common experience to cherish. To make this experience truly memorable, it had to relate to a happy time in all our lives and retrospective happiness invariably finds its seat in youth. Yes, we were going to share the happiest days of our youth with each other and thereby create the bond that would light up our old age. Youth, happiness, clearly this meant the war.

It was Mathilde who came up with the idea, as far as I recall, but it somehow was in the air: all men should tell what they did during those exciting war years. The host was to go first. He had served under von Paulus at Stalingrad and had spent three years as a POW in the Kazakhstan. The next one to go had served under Jodl in the Ardennes and so it went around the room, some in the *Luftwaffe* under Goering, some quite openly in the SS and all were proud of what they had done. One SS man, who had served in Poland, recounted the killing of seven Lublin Jews in as many days. He told it as one big joke, he was particularly proud of Thursday's kill "we made that rat crawl on all fours into a pit of snakes even more poisonous than he." We all laughed at his tale and Mathilde passed the *sekt*. *"Prosit"* intoned our host and we all got up and joined him in a loud unison *"prosit"*.

As we sat down, it was my Gabriel's turn. I was very worried, was he going to confess? If these people found out that we were Jewish, they'd run us out of town. No, Gabriel had used the time the others were telling their stories to make up his own. As a German from the Romanian Banat, he had the choice between the Eastern Front and Africa where physicians were in high demand. In medical school he had taken a course in tropical medicine and this qualified him for service in Rommel's Africa Corps. Now strictly speaking, the Sahara is not quite your typical tropical terrain, but then my Gabriel knew a thing or two about antidotes for snake venoms as well, and that made him particularly useful to Rommel. He had personally accompanied the great Field Marshal on his march to Cairo. The most remarkable instance was their stopover at a desert inn owned by an Egyptian. He had a beautiful French chambermaid, Mouche was her name, and she was working for the British as it turned out and therefore had to be shot. To hear Gabriel tell it, the debacle of El Alamein was all Mouche's fault. Fortunately none of these good German patriots had seen von Stroheim and Anne Baxter do their shtick even once, let alone seven times as I have, or they would have known that Billy Wilder never cast my Gabriel in that movie. After Gabriel's story we all went home, no one could possibly trump that.

On the drive home I took Gabriel to task, what if even one of these people wises up and realizes what he had done, we are cooked. "Not so fast" my Gabriel countered, "not so fast!" He could always claim he meant the whole thing as a joke, just like the SS man and his seven Lublin Jews. Spending the war in an American movie, even if only figuratively, is less of a transgression than throwing Jews in snake pits. "Don't worry, none of this is going to get around." He was right, I needn't have worried, these people had no interest in hurting us. They may have had their suspicions, but ultimately they had fully accepted us, we belonged.

If you think of it, what Gabriel had done was the right thing. We have one big secret, we are bogus Catholic *Auslandsdeutsche,* the big lie of our life my son calls it, maybe he is right. This secret must be preserved at all cost, and if you have a big secret to preserve you are entitled to create new secrets, yes, lies I should call them. The sole purpose of these lies is precisely the preservation of the big secret. You are always allowed to add a new lie, you are just never allowed to get rid of one. The lies must all be consistent, the new lies must buttress the old. Ultimately you are creating your own history and that is your prerogative, as long as everything remains consistent and no contradictions arise. I don't care what my son says, I am the only one in charge of my life, no one else has a say.

There is but one danger, as time goes by, my memory begins to fail me, and I am afraid I will carelessly land in the ultimate contradiction, visible to one and all. Gabriel, he is happily buried in hallowed ground, but I have to carry on without contradiction. Occasionally I do not know any longer who I am. Yes I am Jewish, of course I know that, my father lies buried in a Jewish cemetery somewhere in Romania and I am my father's daughter. But I am also my husband's widow and he slept at an inn on his way to Cairo with Stroheim and Anne Baxter, or maybe he made that up, or maybe my father made his Jewishness up, maybe those weren't phylacteries he was wearing when he said his morning prayer wrapped in his tallis, and maybe that wasn't a tallis after all, but a silk shawl. Who am I to tell? All I know is we got one hundred thousand marks from the German government and therefore now I can live happily in the charming Bavarian town of Dachau awaiting to meet my maker. Many others before me have been brought here to meet that same maker. Maybe they were Jews, or were they Catholics? Who knows? Does it matter?

RATIONAL EXPECTATIONS

I always based my life on what economists call rational expectations: if something is not likely to happen, you need not worry, a modicum of care and foresight will always forestall disaster. It's a foolproof strategy I thought, anyway until today. It still makes no sense to me, no sense at all. Here I am in Zurich and I stay at the Baur au Lac. That alone should exclude my running into almost anyone. Yes, maybe some American CEO, some royalty, a duke here or there and possibly a few Arab sheiks, you pass them in the lobby, you nod and everyone goes his way, no questions asked. But then, my hair isn't crew cut, my blood is not blue, and I never had any dealings with Arabs, so what do I care. Why on earth would the president of the city council of a Romanian city have dealt with Arab sheiks? And after all, that was my business until some years ago, I was the president of the city council of Timişoara, the country's second city, its most cultured and refined, little Vienna they used to call it. And now this! He stays at my hotel and has business at the same investment bank where I keep my assets. Is a meteorite going to strike me on the way to dinner tonight?

It was all so long ago, I wouldn't even have recognized him, he's almost bald and sports a gray beard now. When I last set eyes on him, he was a handsome young man on his road to great things, who would have thought we'd ever meet again? To be honest, it was neither his doing nor mine, anyway not directly. I shouldn't have taken my wife to Johannes Wolf's, I don't know what possessed me, vanity I guess, I wanted Viorica to see how they treat me there. Johannes Wolf's is after all the biggest private investment

45

bank on the Bahnhoffstrasse and I have been dealing with them for over a quarter of a century. Viorica never had any respect for my line of work, she never said so outright, but she never asked any questions, she never showed the slightest interest or understanding, she just always took the flow of money for granted. Occasionally, when I questioned one of her more extravagant purchases, she would start laughing, and teasing me "so sell a few rubies, or emeralds, you haven't sold them all yet, have you?" Now she wants a Piaget wristwatch built into a diamond bracelet. That's big money, three hundred thousand Swiss francs. Say she gets mugged, it's gone, all of it. In France I can't insure the blasted thing, they'd ask questions about the money. Where does it come from? Why was it not declared? Before you know it, I'd languish in a jail on some rock in the sea, like the Count of Monte Cristo. And Viorica, she'd be lost without me. Her degree is in pharmacology. In Romania she taught at the University, I got her the job, and now in Paris she is a researcher at one of the lesser branches of the Sorbonne, not that I ever dare tell her that I am aware of that. Let's just say, we do not live off her salary, that would not even buy a gold-plated Japanese watch.

Purchasing the Piaget, also here on the Bahnhoffstrasse, is a big deal, so I decided to make it into a one-of-a-kind festive occasion and for the first time ever I took Viorica to Johannes Wolf's. Herr Wehrli, the man in charge of my account, received me with great effusiveness and respect, the way one is meant to receive someone who matters. As a rule I give him a "present" each time I come to the bank, a hundred Swiss francs, or occasionally somewhat more, like when he tells me he just had a child, so far he has had six, must be catholic. True we had to wait a little, but the personage admitted ahead of us was an Arab wearing a white gown like a Saudi prince, with one of those red halos on his head. He was accompanied by three likewise attired young men, probably his bodyguards. The message to Viorica was quite clear: Saudi princes and former senior city officials from Timişoara.

So far it all went just as I had planned. Herr Wehrli wanted to give us a cashier's check and we were just leaving his office, to have the check cut, when Viorica asked me in Romanian why we couldn't have the amount in cash. I told her that was not how it is done, but she would have none of it, she had always been a strictly cash shopper "What kind of a bank is this anyway? I haven't seen a teller anywhere. This can't be serious. You should take the money elsewhere, they are going to steal all of it" Suddenly she had become an expert in high finance. Fortunately it was all said in Romanian and I could avoid any embarrassment with an understanding smile, which disparagingly conveyed to the Swiss staff the word "women."

It was at this tense moment that a customer waiting in the hall for his account executive, who was probably taking care of some Arab sheik, jumped up from his seat and embraced me and Viorica *"Domnul Cojocaru, Doamnă"* and he kissed Viorica's hand. It was clear this man knew us, he was speaking fluent Romanian. I smiled. Yes, it was he. "We must get together. I am staying at the Baur au Lac, why don't you come over? Let's go out for dinner and catch up after all these years. What do you say?" What could we say? I was speechless, but Viorica agreed right away "Yes, how about this evening at seven in the lobby, we also stay there. So nice to see you Robbie, you look well." What was that about? I didn't know they had ever met. On the way to the Piaget store she told me that in her days as a practicing pharmacist, in the early years of our marriage, Robbie Fein had been her customer. Wasn't he a just a kid then? "No, my dear, I sold him his first condom, his face was flush red with embarrassment, he was quite cute at fourteen years of age, if that much." OK, a condom, a first condom at that, can be a strong bond between a man and a woman, but still there was my business with Robbie and his family and that could spell financial ruin for me. Rational expectations where are you when we need you?

After all, I didn't do anything so out of the ordinary. The Feins wanted to leave Romania. Who didn't? They were Jews, they *could* go, not like the rest of us stuck up to our necks in the Communist mud. Jews always have a way out, don't they? I tried to help. I netted a handsome profit, I don't deny it, but think of it this way, they couldn't have taken their jewels and silver with them anyway. So the government didn't get it, *I* got it instead, what's so wrong with that? They say it was extortion. True I had to put the squeeze on some of them, they were not going to surrender their valuables willingly, but in the end I came through for them, I delivered.

You see, when Jews got their exit visa it was valid for three days, not a minute longer. They had to liquidate their assets in that short time. Part of that meant surrendering their apartment to the Socialist State the sole owner of all apartments, no such thing as private ownership in a socialist society. They couldn't get their visa to hand till the city certified that they had surrendered their apartment in good condition. The mayor put the city council in charge of making the final inspections and issuing the certificates.

The city council, that was *me*. So I immediately came up with a test case. Right at the beginning there was this obnoxious Jew, one Adalbert Iagolnitzer. I asked for a modest personal fee, but he refused. So I put a hold on his certificate and by the time I issued it to him, his visa had expired and he had no apartment, no belongings *and* no visa. In other words, he was an unemployed homeless person in Socialist Romania and within the year that meant hard labor camp for him. That put the fear of God into that lot. From there on I could name my price and they paid up like lambs. In return they got their certificates in time to have their visas issued so they could leave. What more could they have asked for? Ah, there were tens of thousands of them. As I said, I made a bundle and I am not ashamed. Some way or other I got it all out myself to Zurich, here it was sold and the proceeds deposited at Johannes Wolf's. When my account reached a respectable size, I took Viorica and together we came to represent the city of Timişoara at the European tulip show in Zurich. We didn't win a prize, but we didn't return to Romania either. No, we went on to Paris. I speak no German, but like most educated Romanians I am fluent in French and I like *la vie Parisienne.*

But now if this gets out, oh God! *Doamne Dumnezeule! Sacré Bleu!* I bet you that's why he's here, for revenge. He wants to shake me down, that filthy Jew! Why else would he be staying at the same hotel, and visiting the same investment banker. He wants my money. Here there's nothing I can threaten him with. And there is Viorica. She has a vague idea where all this money comes from, but she knows no details. She never asked a single question, I guess she doesn't want to know, why would she? And yet, all those rubies and emeralds, she is no fool, and now she *needs* a Piaget buried in sparklers. I shouldn't have brought her along, I should have left her in Paris, come over for the day, gone to Wehrli got the money, bought the Piaget and back to Paris. Yes? And then they find it on me at customs and I am fried. On a woman's wrist they let it pass, probably paste they say.

And now he wants to have dinner with us. Why doesn't he just name his price like I did back then? He wants a million? Fine! Let's be done with it! He wants ten million? So be it! But let's get it over with! For God's sake!

To run into Cojocaru, that scumbag, at Johannes Wolf's, I never expected that. But then on second thought, why not? Is he any worse than those Arab sheiks you see there these days. Swiss banks have a knack for attracting the very clientele you worry they might be attracting. They offer them the privacy of numbered accounts and when they drop dead, the Swiss pocket the money. That's how they fleeced the Jews after the war, now it's the Arabs' turn.

At least his wife was with him, Doamna Viorica. I had lost my virginity to her and I am forever in her debt. She was beautiful in those days, she had all the piquancy and sensuality only a Romanian woman has, not even French women come close. From the junk clothes then available in the stores, she instinctively knew how to create an attire you just wanted to tear off her, as you lost yourself in her voluptuous body. I went to her pharmacy to purchase a condom. My friends had impressed upon me the importance of some home-work on condom-use, lest I be caught unawares when I needed it for real and thereby become everyone's laughing stock. I had just turned thirteen, I remember learning about the importance of condoms at Mr. Kauftheil's, waiting with the other boys learning the haphtarah for our bar mitzvahs.

"Is it for your own use?" Doamna Viorica inquired, while looking me over.

"Erh .... Yes" I muttered .

"Hm" and she disappeared in the backroom. A minute later she reappeared "My ladder is broken, you are taller than I, want to give me a hand?" Nervously I followed her into the backroom. She pointed to the shelf on which the rubbers were kept and as I tried to reach it on tiptoes, she offered me her help by supporting my crotch with her left hand. This had a predictable effect on me and without having un-shelved a single prophylactic, we took a rest in each other's arms. A quarter of an hour later, with six condoms in my pocket, I was leaving the pharmacy without the virginity I had still possessed when setting foot in it.

Over the following weeks we had many more installments of these delights, but it all ended one time with us in the backroom and Cojocaru paying a visit to his young wife. When hearing his voice, we joined him fast in front, and Doamna Viorica pressed a bottle of some kind of pills in my hand "Tell your mother to take two before each meal. I hope she gets well soon." I promised I would, and I left in a hurry, buttoning the last button on my fly. I don't know whether Cojocaru noticed anything, but in those days I worried he might have and I put a stop to my, by then frequent, visits to Doamna Viorica's pharmacy.

He must have noticed something I thought, when he treated us to that bizarre charade two days before our exit visa was to expire. Even though this was six years later, I was always convinced that this was Cojocaru's revenge for my having dallied with his wife. Barely had my parents and I been notified that we had been granted visas to leave the country due to expire three days hence, than my uncle Sanyi showed up at our place with an air of deep mystery radiating from his wide open blue eyes. A friend of his had handed uncle Sanyi a list from Cojocaru of the items he wanted as payment for the apartment surrender certificate. Should we fail to comply, Cojocaru would see to it that we do penance in the company of Adalbert Iagolnitzer in a hard labor camp. Cojocaru's list was very specific: the five kilo silver tray used at our New Year's eve party the year the war had ended, the diamond and sapphire brooch my mother had worn at Annie Fischer's piano recital at the opera house three seasons ago and so on it went. I just wonder where he came by all this information, but it was clear he had some first rate sources. We knew there was no room for error and filled two old leather suitcases with the demanded items.

As soon as night had settled, uncle Sanyi and I, both outfitted in trench coats and fedoras, were briskly walking towards the part of town where the streets were named after French and Italian cities, the unreach-able destinations of everyone's dreams in that sad country. In the drizzle the wet cobblestones were shining under the flickering weak streetlights. Uncle Sanyi was walking ahead and I was trying to keep up with him while carrying the larger and much heavier of the two suitcases. At the corner of Paris and Milan uncle Sanyi stopped, took the heavy suitcase from me, looked around to make sure no one had seen us, and after sign-aling that I should wait for him, turned the corner. I paced up and down Paris, and barely two minutes later, uncle Sanyi rejoined me, a big smile on his face, mission accomplished! It all felt eerily out of a French movie, only Jean Gabin and Bourvil were missing. In lock step we started on our way back.

Next day the inspector arrives. After the customized bribe Cojocaru had already received, we had every right to expect this to go smoothly, a mere formality. But this young inspector, an unusually handsome fellow, is starting to make trouble, a spot on the wall here, a scratch on the door there, to any reasonable person normal wear and tear, but not to this public servant. "I am sorry but all this will have to be taken care of first, and I could return for a final inspection say a week from today" So after all those trays and brooches Iagolnitzer's fate was awaiting us. At this point my mother, on the assumption "like boss, like aide" walks over to the young inspector and places a substantial amount of cash in his hand

"I think this should cover all the repairs. This way could we get the apartment surrender certificate to hand today?"

"Comrade, you are attempting to bribe a public official. I have to confiscate this money and report this attempted corruption of a public servant to the authorities. For your information, this is a felony, a very serious matter. Good day to you."

Goodbye Iagolnitzer, we won't be joining you in your hard labor camp after all. No! We're headed directly for a high security prison with state of the art torture chambers. By the time we get to see again the eternally hopeful rays of the sun, to hear again the lovely song of the nightingale, we will be shadows of our former selves, waiting for the grim reaper to come and relieve us from our torments.

This is the time at which recriminations start and just as we thought we had finally succeeded in fairly apportioning the blame, the phone rang and a woman in a most monotonous voice identified herself as Cojocaru's secretary and asked for me and me *alone* to immediately come to his office at City Hall. Where horror and premonitions of unspeakable evil had held forth a moment earlier, three smiles out of nowhere landed on the faces of the three occupants of this room. There was still hope, after all!

I was admitted to the City Council President's office without any wait. The young inspector was there with the kind of expression on his face docile servants use to convey outrage, when they are certain that is what their superior expected of them.

"Comrade Fein, this good public servant just reported to me about your mother's outrageous attempt to bribe him" at this the handsome inspector started waving the wad of bills given him by my mother. "What have you to say to this comrade?"

"I am as outraged as this honorable public servant is at my mother's intolerable behavior. I should add though that given the momentous succession of events of the past twenty four hours" and I looked Cojocaru straight in the eyes "my mother, I am afraid, has taken leave of her senses. In the name of my whole family I therefore would like to apologize to this vigilant official of the socialist state and to assure him that such disgusting patterns of behavior will never again be engaged in by any of us."

"I approve of your self-criticism, comrade" now Cojocaru turned to the visibly moved inspector , "and I suggest to you to accept this apology, about the sincerity of which I do not have the slightest doubt."

Thus encouraged by his boss, the inspector took a few steps in my direction, I followed his initiative and started approaching him as well. We met in front of Cojocaru. The inspector now moved the money from his right to his left hand and the two of us forcefully shook hands. His hand was sweating profusely and not having been washed while the inspector was on duty, it felt outright sticky. Without asking what should now happen to the bribe money he was holding, the inspector put that money in his pocket and thereby fully closed the matter in what to his eyes was a truly fair and honorable manner. Cojocaru presently signaled to the inspector that his presence was no longer required and the young man left the room.

With only the two of us standing in the big office, Cojocaru motioned with both hands toward the walls, to remind me that like all offices, this majestic room was bugged. With great solemnity he then said,

"Comrade Fein, you and you parents have elected to leave our country in order to rejoin your loved ones abroad. Family reunification is a worthy cause deeply respected by a socialist state like ours, which operates according to the highest humanitarian principles. Unlike you, I for one have decided to stay in my fatherland and participate to the extent of my abilities in the noblest of all causes, the building of communism. Should fate ordain that we meet again at some time in the future, I hope you will recall what transpired here today." He walked to his desk, signed the certificate and handed it to me. "Good bye comrade, good luck and as I said, *remember.*"

Prophetic words. You needn't worry Mr. Comrade Cojocaru, I have not forgotten. You could have spared us that charade, but what's over is over, I am not the vengeful type. Of course you have no way of knowing that, and I can just imagine how you must feel right now and to be frank that pleases me no end. Dinner tonight promises to be a lot of fun in its own cathartic way.

I have been with Johannes Wolf's for over thirty-seven years now. I still have my little house in Oerlikon and take the train to town every morning. I don't put on airs now that I am a senior account executive. Things have changed around here over the years. It used to be, we had to deal mostly with European clients, Frenchmen and Germans securing their assets from the reach of the taxman, English lords on their way to Italy, and of course the Jews. Before the war we had many Jewish-owned accounts. Kurt Fraunfelder, my mentor, used to tell me about the numbered account of a Mr. Funk from Bratislava, a department store owner. He had a good thirty million dollars in his account. After the Germans marched in, Herr Funk found it appropriate to make his way to Switzerland where his money was — Jews always head for the money like moths for the flame. They turned Herr Funk away at the border, he had no valid visa. He insisted that the guards contact Johannes Wolf's to confirm his story. The guards did contact us, but for obvious reasons he didn't give them the account number and according to our secrecy in banking laws we could not even admit that he had an account with us, let alone indicate its balance. He was turned back at the border and that was the last he we heard of him. What did these Jews think? Just having dollars in Zurich gave them some moral right to come to live among us as if their ancestors hadn't murdered our Lord? After the war the account remained inactive for over ten years at which point its balance was transferred to our bank. This basic strategy was used in many other cases as well and proved very lucrative. Frauenfelder was promoted. There were some complications later on, but that's another matter, by then my mentor was a wreck in the wake of two severe strokes.

With these Arabs it's the same thing. They all go for the numbered account and when they die, their money becomes ours to keep. We have nothing against the Arabs, just as we had nothing against the Jews. The Arabs hadn't even had a hand in killing our Lord. How could they? That prophet of theirs hadn't even been born yet.

Today this Saudi man with his bodyguards wanted to buy yellow metallic gold coins with the millions he had made on the black gold spewing forth in his desert backyard. I offered him our numismatically so much sought after Swiss Vreneli, but he wouldn't hear of it. Why? Because Swiss gold has the Confederation's symbol, the Swiss cross, on its back. For this Saudi count, or prince, or whatever, this meant the crusades all over again and he would have none of it. He went for the numismatically worthless

French Napoleon. Little does *he* know what that Corsican thug did to his Egyptian Arab brothers. He just liked the laurels on the emperor's head, probably thought he was some Roman emperor before the birth of the Prophet. They don't teach about the French in the sands of Arabia.

And then there are these Romanians, Christians of the Eastern kind, might as well be pagans if you ask me. Where does their money come from? That's none of my business, really. Take this Cojocaru fellow, used to always come alone but today found it necessary to bring his wife along, an aging hussy supposedly badly in need of a three hundred thousand franc Piaget watch with diamonds and God knows what else! If I was her husband I'd buy her a gold-plated Japanese Casio and watch over her like an Othello. She even gave *me* the sweet eye. Romanian women! There you are! At least the Cojocarus live in Paris and not in our neck of the woods. It's such a relief to return to Oerlikon every evening to the wholesome meal prepared for me by Vreni, my wife of thirty years, alas no children. All I ever bought her was a chrome Schaffhausen ladies' watch for our silver wedding anniversary. Time will be time. Diamonds and gold can't change that.

Yes, my life is tranquil and fulfilled, but even so, every now and then a deep unease settles over me. I guess it must be a kind of disgust with what all these Arabs and Jews and Romanians are up to. I cannot afford letting myself wallow in the blues, so I have found a way of coping with them. On the second day after the blues' onset, at noon, instead of going with my colleagues for lunch at Sprüngli's across the street, I claim personal business and walk down to the railway station, cross the Limmat and in an old house on the third floor there is a salon where they have the remedy for what ails me. I repair to a private room, I undress, I lie on my stomach on the massage table and then the attendant enters the room, starts shouting at me, gets the leather belt and starts whipping my buttocks. It fires me up, the fear makes me wet the sheet, but they don't mind, it's expected they assure me, no need for embarrassment, the hygienic standards of this establishment are impeccable. I leave a reconstructed man, eager to perform the demanding duties of a Swiss banker.

There was a weird scene in the lobby today, I wonder what it portends. Another client — a man by the name of Fein, I've seen him around from time to time — greeted Cojocaru and his Piaget-bound wife in the lobby as if they were old friends. I had always pegged this Fein for a Frenchman, of course of the Mosaic faith with a name like that, but he apparently speaks fluent Romanian. Yet his French is unaccented. These Jews! They dissimulate forever. He even wears a beret, as if he were coming directly from the set of some French movie or other. Why could he not give his native accent free rein when he speaks what for him must be a foreign language. No Swiss would ever want to deceive that way. French is one of our four official languages, but we are not ashamed of our accents, by speaking out we affirm our identity and we do not wear berets for show. We earn our money the hard way, and we put in many hours of thoroughly honest work, we don't go in for get-rich-quick schemes like these Romanians, these Arabs, these Jews. Let them quarrel with each other, let them fight, let them kill each other, they are asking for it.

———————————

Finally I am alone for a moment. Cojocaru went down for breakfast, it's included, God forbid he should miss it, that man can be such a cheapskate. I am trying to recover after last night. We went to a place just out of town by the lake, elegant, discreet, expensive. From the way Robbie was looking at me, it was clear he was no longer attracted to me. Gone was any sexual interest, not once did he attempt to establish even the most perfunctory physical contact. He was more interested in hearing what Cojocaru had to say than in savoring even for an ever so brief moment the memories of his initiation into the rituals of ecstasy, the rituals that make this life on earth worth living. It couldn't have been my dress or my jewels, I even took the Piaget on its first outing. He probably thought it was gaudy paste stuck onto an old hag to distract from the ravages of time. Have I really changed *that* much? Can my décolletage no longer stir the groins of men? Does a smile on my face just add more wrinkles to those chiseled permanently on it? Robbie was aloof, worse, he was outright cold, as if not wishing to be bothered. It was hard getting used to.

Even Robbie has aged, he is balding, has grown a graying beard, but somehow men have sold us a false bill of goods. Carve a wrinkle on a man's forehead and you are immediately instructed to see wisdom and manliness along its deep track, he is all the more desirable for it. Do the same to a woman and her stock plummets to all but the blind. It just isn't fair.

Cojocaru was very nervous, he stalled the Jew with lies, simple lies. Nobody suspects it, but I really know all there is to know about how the

Feins were shaken down by my husband. He never told me himself, he firmly believes that I am impervious to all this. But the truth, as always, has many more facets. This was years after Robbie had been my lover. What was I to do, settle for a man whose one pleasure in life comes from the metallic sound of gold coins scooped out of a box and then slowly trickled back through the chink between two palms? There are many pleasures in life: thinking up a powerful new idea, doing something for the greater good, enjoying great works of art, to name but a few. I know full well that my ideas have not had much of an impact, and to be frank, I can't think of anything I have ever done for the greater good. Oh, I like to go to a museum, a theatre, a concert hall, a movie house. Occasionally I enjoy a well-written book, but not by a long shot could I claim that any of these activities gives me the pleasure I most crave in life. If there is one overriding pleasure, one which I could honestly claim to be the dream that keeps me alive, it is seeing a man get aroused as he sets eyes on me, and then yielding to his hot desire and letting myself be invaded by his passion to the point of frenzy where he and I become one and nature rewards us with her supreme delight.

Cojocaru is obviously not the man I have in mind. I always had to find another. Robbie was one, and what he gave me was his youthful innocence, which left no place for the fakeries of the experienced male. It did not last. Cojocaru caught us in the act once, though he was sufficiently distracted and lacking in interest, not to understand what he had seen. Robbie left in a state of total agitation, which didn't register with my husband. When he later went on to shake down the Feins, he wasn't even aware that Robbie was the very boy he had seen that day in the pharmacy where I was working. I know this for a fact, for at that later time the man in my life was Cojocaru's assistant, the fellow who threatened to denounce Mrs. Fein for attempted bribery. He was a handsome man, not innocent like Robbie, but still aware of what matters in life. He told me about the Fein's apartment surrender certificate while we were making love. With eyes closed he was lying on his back while I was sitting astride him. He started telling me the story, then in the throes of passion stopped. When he got what he was after, he fell asleep, then later as he combed his hair before leaving me, he finished his tale.

I had always suspected something, there had to be one activity that kept Cojocaru going, and it was enriching himself in whatever way possible.

He had been entrusted with a power and he abused it to the hilt. How he got the money out to Zurich, I have no idea, even his handsome aide was in the dark about that. But that is irrelevant, anyway as far as I am concerned. With me he always behaved like a gentleman. He accommodated my every whim, he helped my career, or so we thought at the time. Without him I would never have left the backroom of the pharmacy for the classroom. Teaching pharmacology was hardly what should have been in the cards for me. Give me mortar and pestle over chalk and blackboard any day. I was much happier mixing lotions and preparing ointments while not knowing who next might walk into my pharmacy and how they thought of attaining earthly happiness. But we do not get to see the path to happiness; that all is wrapped in mystery and more often than not we take the wrong turn and get to see the dead end only when we come to it. In retrospect, the forks in the road all acquire blaring signs in language comprehensible to us, but at first encounter it is all a game of chance. I should never have married that man, I should have settled for some handsome young fellow whose search for happiness led him to my body. Do I really need a Piaget wristwatch encrusted with diamonds? In Romania I had never heard even the name of that brand, let alone its price. Yet now I derive a certain sick form of pleasure fastening its cold diamonds to my wrist and Cojocaru seems to derive genuine pleasure from this perversion of mine. Yet a man whose virginity was lost inside my body does not even notice this gaudy timepiece.

We sat down at the restaurant and Cojocaru right away started holding forth. For my illumination both men started reconstructing the facts as accurately as they could from what they had once known and now tried to summon from their memory. It didn't occur to either of them that I might know as much as they did and then some, for I knew also how being made love to by the very teller of the tale feels.

To their minds the fundamental question was whether the aide's denunciation threats were meant honestly or as part of a scheme to provide some after-the-fact justification for what was no more than your basic shakedown. Neither man would even think of raising the possibility that a payment was extracted to right a wrong. Cojocaru had never admitted even to himself that a wrong had ever been committed by the Fein boy, the one he then summoned to City Hall. That boy and the teenager leaving my pharmacy that afternoon were two different creatures in Cojocaru's mind, and even had they merged, he would not have found any cause for alarm.

In my regard Cojocaru had never acted proprietary, as if sharing me with another man were something of no serious consequence to him. I cannot imagine Robbie not having entertained the thought that he was reaping Cojocaru's long due revenge. But now, Robbie is a happy man in a free world, a respected French jurist, married with three daughters. Why would he bother to dredge up the past? He met us, we had dinner and the matter will soon be forgotten. Paris is a big city, there's space for all three of us to live our lives, to coexist as they say. Fathers don't tell their daughters how their virginity was lost, that's not a subject fit for the ears of impressionable young girls.

I could blow all of this sky high, a major scandal, adultery, extortion, numbered Swiss accounts. For that matter what business can a respected French jurist have these days with the folks who invented money laundering? And yet I said nothing, I just let the two men play their game and in the end feel they both had won. Robbie never played his trump card, he did not demand restitution of the extorted goods. Cojocaru did not bring up the equally inflammatory matter of the unbuttoned fly. The extortionist got to keep his millions, the adulterer his reputation. Then they parted ways.

But where does all this leave me? In front of the mirror I guess, spending my time applying ointments and lotions to my countenance in between ever more frequent face lifts. And men? As of late I started paying for their services. At first it was an expensive gift to a well-built stud, rewarded for a round of passionate lovemaking. Then the currency had to shed its euphemisms and for some months now I have been paying in cash. It simplifies things and if you are generous from the start, there won't be any of that ugly haggling. Men who know how to please a woman, be it even for a high price, know how to endow the sexual transaction with a certain dignity. Slowly I'll have the Piaget stones replaced with glass, Cojocaru won't be the wiser, then I'll sell the diamonds and buy me the handsomest Rive Gauche man money can buy. I am not a jurist and for me the sound of gold coins trickling through the chink between two palms is just that, gilded clanking.

A STABBING PAIN

The other day, I ran into Schatzi Taussig on Washington Square. She had lost so much weight, I barely recognized her. The trademark seductive smile was still sitting on her lips after all these years, but she was no longer the *zaftig* woman I remembered from her days as Dr. Taussig's fourth wife. Shortly after the doctor's death — he had a heart attack on Loga row, one of the more beautiful residential streets of Timişoara — Schatzi managed to get out of Romania and had settled at a "fabulously" wealthy aunt's place in Australia. Her aunt had died since, and the fabulous wealth — a "chain" of three kosher butcheries in Melbourne — was now Schatzi's.

At a café in the Village we started recalling old times and catching up on recent ones. After all this time, our friendship was coming to life again and I mustered the courage to inquire about her shapely figure. I expected it to be related to some stipulation in her aunt's will: "if she weighs in at more than 150 pounds then the butcheries go to the state of Israel . . ." No, it wasn't anything like that. Schatzi's face darkened as if an infinite horror had taken three-dimensional shape and plopped down beside her. Gone was the smile, as she prepared to talk about something she had obviously kept bottled up for years. "You were there, you might understand," she started. "I have lived with it in frustration and shame, but maybe *you* will understand me."

"You remember *seliger* Moritz", a bilingual reference to her late husband. "The year he died things got really bad for us. True, we had what to eat and we had a two-room flat, which was a great thing in those days, but surveillance grew very intense. You could tell a *spitzel* from a regular

59

patient. They never minded to wait, indeed, you'd think they had come just to do that. They were polite, they would give up their turn to patients who arrived after them, and invariably, they would complain about the hard times in front of total strangers. I need not explain to you, of all people, that this was not kosher."

Indeed, I only too well remembered those times, when you only complained to your mother or to your father, and even that in an empty open space. *Spitzels,* that mainstay of the communist regime, were rudely listening in on street conversations. They would drop something next to you and keep picking it up until they got the gist of what was being said. At home the telephone serviceman would come so often to "repair" the functional instrument, that it was only too obvious, what went wrong was the bug it contained. This was hardly surprising, for the phone itself was from the good old days when the phone company had been American-owned, while with its weak economy, Romania could hardly afford Western surveillance equipment, and had to rely on the home-made, or even worse, on the Russian-made product.

"Yes," she went on, "when a *spitzel* got in to Moritz, he invariably would have some nondescript ailment, would refuse any medication, above all injections, and would end up paying with a brand new 50 Lei bill. We were used to this at the rate of one *spitzel* or two a week, but now we had a regular invasion: at any moment there was one in waiting. They always wanted Moritz to give them brand-name Swiss or American antibiotics, which you could purchase only on the black market. It was obvious they were up to something. Put on the pressure, get us to make a wrong move and off to jail we go. I was Moritz' nurse and would warn him each time by somehow or other incorporating the word 'lemon' when introducing the patient to him. This, because once we had a *spitzel*, one Izidor Citrom, who in the old days used to sell insurance to my father and who, overcome by embarrassment at meeting me, admitted his real function. I remember I let him keep his 50 Lei bill but he insisted I change it to a used one, or else they would suspect him.

"It was in the middle of all this on a Friday night. We had just finished a hard day, ten hours, some forty patients, including five or six *spitzels*, and were counting out the day's cash intake as the phone rang. It was Doamna Vladimirescu, the one who lived by the river."

"Yes," I interjected, "her grandson went to school with me, Radu was his name, wasn't it?"

"That's right," she went on, "Moritz had grown up in that neighborhood himself, in fact only two houses away, so he could hardly turn her down when in the most alarmed of voices she literally begged him to come out and see her nephew who was suddenly taken very ill, it sounded like food poisoning."

"Did the Vladimireasca have a nephew?" I asked, surprised, though aware that time may have scrambled my memories. Schatzi paid no attention, she had a story to tell and would not tolerate interruptions.

"Moritz had a quick sandwich, a beer, and then caught the first tram to the Vladimireasca's home, There, he was mysteriously led to a small maid's room. A 30-Watt bulb provided all the lighting, but it was clear that the patient had hepatitis, he was very yellow. So Moritz told them it's unpleasant but curable, and urged immediate hospitalization, infectious hepatitis was highly contagious after all. At this point the patient whose name was, wouldn't you know, Tudor — yes, Tudor Vladimirescu like the legendary 1821 rebel — protested. He could not check into a hospital, he said, he was on the run from the *Securitate*. If he surfaced they would do him in. Moritz would have loved not to have been told all this. Not reporting a case of infectious disease was an offense, but hardly a major one, milder I would say than purchasing auromycin on the black market, but shielding a fugitive, a politico, from the security police, meant in fact becoming a politico oneself. Moritz pretended not to have understood what had just been said, but there were witnesses, the Vladimireasca and her daughter, and he knew it. He said something like 'I'll see to it' and left.

Back home, in a state of total agitation and terror, he agonized and agonized. Was this a *superspitzel* for whom they had warmed him up with the increased surveillance, or was this for real? If it was a provocation and he did not denounce the patient, he was in essence signing his and my arrest warrants. Yes, mine too, because they wouldn't have believed he hadn't told me. I told him so be it, but he continued agonizing. After all, there was the surveillance, there was the peculiar name of the nephew, and there was the fact that he did not remember *either*" at this word she nodded in my direction "about the Vladimireasca having a nephew." So I had been right after all, she had heard my question, I had but asked it in the wrong place.

"His agitation grew and we rehashed the details over and over. Maybe he could pretend not to have understood, but then again, there were the witnesses. He was an old man, but I would also suffer. He even contemplated suicide. As it dawned, I made him a very strong coffee, he got up, combed himself, added a large dose of brilliantine as if worried that even his hair might not cooperate in what he was about to do, and set out on foot to the *Securitate* headquarters, you remember, they were on the beautiful Loga row and there was no tram line there.

"He was received by a very polite captain who immediately knew the man Moritz was talking about." Schatzi was speaking with total abandon now. Peripheral as her own part in it may have been, this was still very much her story.

"They told Moritz to wait and presently the captain returned with four more *Securitate* men and informed Moritz that they would go to arrest the patient. They made it all the more realistic by warning Moritz that this patient was heavily armed and most dangerous. A plan was agreed upon and then carried out. Moritz rang the bell, entered the apartment, and was preparing an injection for the sick man. As he stood with the syringe in his hand, the *Securitate* agents burst into the room with pulled guns and everybody, including Moritz, was ordered to hold their hands up. They allowed Moritz to give the injection and then arrested the lot of them. After they carried off the patient, they escorted Moritz, patted him on the shoulder, and most politely took their leave. They might as well have shot him there and then. He came home exhausted. He had no appetite, he refused to see patients, he was silent. Guilt and fear of immense proportions inscribed themselves on his forehead, as if his name had suddenly been changed to Cain.

"In the afternoon, he got up and said he was going to take a walk. I said I'm coming along, but he insisted on leaving alone. I never saw him alive again. You came to the funeral, didn't you?"

"No, I didn't, I was at college in Bucharest at the time, but I remember hearing about it."

"Fate would have it, later that year, that all the properly placed bribes got me an exit visa and I went directly to my aunt. I have never told this story before because it might cloud his memory, but now, to you..." It was clear that she had told the story so many times to herself, that she had no thoughts or hesitations about its structure. The only difference was, this time she had an audience, the tree was not falling in the empty forest.

"You know, a few years after my arrival in Melbourne, I started having a stabbing pain in my abdomen, they found I had developed ulcers. They cut out two thirds of my stomach, you asked about my figure..." An unaccustomed bitter smile settled on her lips. She wanted me to know that she had paid the price: two thirds of a stomach for the right to finally tell her story.

DIESEL ELECTRICS

In Fifties Romania Renée was a countess in the wrong place at the wrong time. In the old days her aristocratic French father had been so much in love with her mother that for her sake he became a subject of His Majesty King Michael of Romania. He died since in a communist labor camp by the Danube Canal, his fortune confiscated and his Romanian wife bringing up as best she could Renée, the willy-nilly heir to her father's title. Renée studied chemistry at the University of Timişoara, I studied electrical engineering there. I knew I was not meant to be an electrical or any other kind of engineer for that matter, but I loved mathematics, and electrical engineering was where you best studied mathematics in Timişoara. If this sounds weird, keep in mind that Timişoara is not in New Jersey.

I had a friend Ivan Weiss, a tall, thin, nervous fellow. He used to come to our house, go to the piano, pull his small stomach in, and in his light bass start singing arias, mostly Mozart. He was obsessed with ideas of freedom and, my advice to the contrary, kept rambling about what it would take to "implement freedom" in Romania. I remember he would say to anyone willing to listen that "communism has to go." Others tried to warn him that this rambling would come to a bad end, but he just went on with it and after a while we all took it for granted that the authorities had decided not to take him seriously, to let him ramble on as some kind of holy fool. Beyond his ideas of freedom for Romanians, the Jew Ivan Weiss had one other passion. He was madly in love with Renée. She knew it, we all knew it, but she always rejected him, being a countess was bad enough, what more did she need in communist Romania. "Freedom" was hardly a commodity that interested her.

Then one day Ivan disappeared, just like that. It was clear that they had arrested him, for his room had been ransacked and his roommate was questioned for days, before they let him pack his things and ordered him to leave town. Apparently the holy fool had been reclassified as a rabble-rouser. Rumors about leaflets floated all over. Leaflets were the obsession of the communists. Not for nothing did all typewriters have to be registered at the police with new imprints to be taken each year. So now, Ivan Weiss the "leafleteer" had disappeared, and his roommate was sent back to Transylvania whence he had come. No more holy fools. We all got the message.

A few weeks after Ivan Weiss' disappearance, I went to the Student Union where a Saturday night dance was in progress. There I saw, nonchalantly dancing, cold Renée, the beauty who had spurned her gallant Jewish suitor, out of a fear of holy fools or whatever other reasons she may have had. Her light brown hair, her blue eyes, her whole posture made her the most visible dancer. She was whirling with a tall student who matched her good looks, even if he couldn't hold a candle to Renée when it came to intelligence, which radiated from her eyes. It was clear that she was aware of her brains just as she was aware of her good looks. She appeared overwhelmed by a kind of weariness, prey to the fatalism of the person caught in the rapids without a life jacket, going downstream at breakneck speed while still hoping for a miracle. I found this dance outrageous. Poor Ivan in a *Securitate* torture chamber and his knowing idol turning on the dance floor with the business-as-usual attitude of a siren entrapping a sailor. I decided I had to stand up for my friend and, as of the next dance, claimed her as my partner for the rest of the evening. The good-looking dolt settled for less aristocratic companionship.

We spoke not a word. I looked upon my mission as one of punishment, of vengeance. Only much later, as the band was close to folding up, did we exchange a few words. By then we were dancing cheek to perfectly fitting cheek, body to tense sweating body. Vengeance and punishment may be noble as missions, but they are also powerful aphrodisiacs and a shell of desire enveloped our bodies. We left abruptly and walked directly to the Rose Garden by the Bega Canal and from there into the park in which I had played hide and seek as a child. We sat on a bench, but Renée would not make love to me, no way. The pill hadn't made it to this backwater and I had no condom. So now we were *forced* to speak. It turned out she had no interest whatever in Ivan, and had conveyed this immutable fact to him gently but in no uncertain terms. Maybe I had wanted to hear this, for by now I fathomed myself in love with Renée. I held her in my arms and she did not passively accept my embrace, she pulled me closer. We were forming an alliance, "we two" against all else, the countess and the *other* Jew. Ivan, the original Jew, was forgotten by now, as were vengeance and punishment. Tenderness and delight had taken their place.

We next met at my place, which I had to myself, everyone else was gone. But Renée would not come alone. The temptations would be too hard to resist. She brought her best friend Flavia and I my best friend Cornelius Hand, a German boy from Sibiu, we called him Cary. This way we all were protected from ourselves and from each other. By candlelight, youth created an atmosphere of togetherness, of belonging. Nothing happened though, even as there were two rooms with beds in plain view. In the wee hours we escorted the girls back to their dorm and on our way back I remember exchanging a look with Cary which sealed this evening in our memories as the most romantic and happy in our lives. Thereafter, both Renée and Flavia started avoiding us and I have never spoken to either of them since.

Years later, Cary married Renée, yes the countess, not the other one. Cary was a tall blond, very German rugby player who could down thirty-two scrambled eggs in one sitting, but who would faint from three puffs on a Turkish cigar. Cary was a genius. He studied electrical engineering not as a mathematics substitute, as I did, but because he loved, he passionately loved, electrical machines, generators, motors, transformers. Given the task, I could design a transformer for any reasonable situation. There is a logical way of doing this and by mathematical standards, it is reasonably trivial. Given the same task, Cary would just draw a transformer without any calculations whatsoever, then distance himself from his drawing for a minute or two and say, "Yes, this might do it." His specifications would turn out close to those I had arrived at by calculation, the thing would in fact work. But then there were those little touches that made his transformer compare to mine the way a hand-crafted Rolls-Royce compares to a computer-designed Chevy. When we ultimately graduated in 1958, it was clear to both of us that I was headed towards a career in mathematics, he in electrical engineering. The two of us graduated at the top of our class, but we weren't allowed decent jobs, he for being German, I for being Jewish. We were given jobs, of course, but out of the very bottom of the pickings.

We both landed employment in the mountains of Western Transylvania, doing "rural electrification," convincing the peasants about the advantages of electricity. Neither of us went. My uncle knew the Party Secretary in the nearest town and for a modest bribe this good Party member made me redundant even before laying eyes on me. For another installment of the same bribe Cary became as redundant as I had become before him. So here we literally bought ourselves a year of doing what we wanted. I wanted to do mathematics and I did learn a lot that year. Cary, in turn became a volunteer engineer at the big machine factory in Timişoara . Just that year this factory was introducing a new model Diesel-electric engine for Russian consumption, with sale prospects even in the West. To look at the design, it was unmistakably Cary's. It was a work of art, fit for crossing the American prairie.

After one year without official employment Cary became a "parasite" in the communist "legal" sense of that word, and thereby eligible for deportation to a forced labor camp. I managed to get out of Romania three days short of metamorphosing into a parasite. Cary, on the other hand, was arrested and as he could not come up with another job at a moment's notice, was deported to a labor camp in Dobrogea, repairing the Cernavodă bridge over the Danube. It was during his second year at this camp that he reconnected with Renée . She had also become a parasite, understandably so, for no one in Communist Romania would be foolish enough to hire a countess, even one with a degree in chemistry. Unlike Cary, the countess worked in the kitchen and it was over lunch that they met again. They "did lunch" as it were. They were both so lonely that it took no more than one lunch and one dinner before they ended up taking a walk together, as long as feasible within the perimeter of the camp, and in a more isolated spot they made love. They developed a very intense relationship, but not a relationship that grew naturally, rather something obsessive, redemptive and above all something meant to relieve the monotony of camp life.

A few months into this relationship, a commissar was dispatched to the camp to contact Cary. The brilliant original design notwithstanding, the Diesel-electrics were having problems, the workmanship, not supervised by Cary, had been shoddy and the Russians were complaining. Would Cary consider taking the job of engineer on the Diesel-electric project and see to it that these outstanding problems were solved. Cary knew the commissar, one Gheorghe Bucea, a former classmate of ours. This commissar had a degree in electrical engineering, but though in charge of the whole Diesel-electric project, he was totally ignorant in matters technical. His expertise was confined to party discipline, to slogans and to denunciations. He was prospering.

To get out of the labor camp, Cary accepted the Diesel-Electric job on condition that he be allowed to marry Renée and relieve her of parasitism by turning her into a "housewife," an acceptable non-parasitic occupation for a female under communism. Thus Renée and Cary moved back to the town of their studies and went legit. Cary took a good look at the engines delivered to Russia and realized the wiring was all faulty. He designed a way of servicing all these engines which, though costly, could be expeditiously executed to the satisfaction of the powerful customers. He moreover revamped the whole production process, so as to eliminate this problem.

This took about three years, during which Cary and Renée got an apartment in one of the "matchboxes" as the new building blocks on the outskirts of the city were known and settled down in a modicum of comfort. They now for the first time could live, not as hopeless prisoners in a concentration camp, but as lovers. Yet this relationship was not meant for the two of them. Cary was easygoing, Renée passionate. Cary was a dreamer, Renée a realist. Cary wanted children, Renée wanted excitement. As their marriage headed downhill, Cary started drinking. The same physique that readily accommodated thirty-two scrambled eggs, was less sturdy when invaded with thirty-two shots of țuică.

After three years Gheorghe Bucea no longer needed Cary, the Diesel-electrics now worked as designed. Bucea did what he did best, he denounced Cary for "reactionary excesses" and before he could say "parasite," Cary was one again and thereby so was Renée. The fear of labor camp further strained the tenuous sacrament and Cary and Renée were now at it from early morning into the late night, when Cary finally got that "click" that made it all go away.

Ten months later Renée went to Bucea to plead for Cary and of course also for herself. Bucea received her with the kind of subservience *lumpenproletars* instinctively display towards aristocrats. He laughed when Renée told him about her and Cary's predicament, and then, when Renée got her handkerchief to wipe off the tears of humiliation, he proposed a deal, "I want to fuck you Renée." This was the subtle way he put it. Bucea was a light-skinned fellow with gray eyes, he had been quite handsome in his youth, without ever being aware of this fact. He bit his nails to the raw, his fingers were red from soaking in saliva all the time, and for relaxation Gheorghe Bucea masturbated. After graduation he adopted a more dissolute life-style, he no longer used his hands to relieve his inner yearnings, but got female job applicants to take care of his sex life. If the applicant had serious political problems, Gheorghe Bucea did not shy away from rape.

Renée, not ready yet to prostitute herself, got up, realizing that Bucea would not help. It is at this point that Gheorghe Bucea locked the door to his office and started tearing the clothes off Renée. When she continued to resist, Gheorghe Bucea used the gun the Party had issued him and pointed it at Renée's head. She obediently fell to her knees and complied. Before he climaxed, Gheorghe Bucea mounted Renée, the gun issued him by the Party still in his left hand, and then released inside Renée . This is how the countess was impregnated by the *lumpenproletar.*

At this time Cary and Renée 's sex life was limited to memories and when Renée started showing the signs of pregnancy, Cary, not a believer in immaculate conception himself, had to accept the fact that his countess had dabbled in adultery. He coped with this situation by increasing his intake of alcohol so as to achieve a faster "click".

Renée gave birth to a ten-pound little girl with blue eyes and blond hair, and Bucea was undeniably the father. He knew this and would have liked to brag. Renée begged him not to, but all the same he announced at work that Mrs. Hand had born him a daughter, Viorica. Cary was reduced to a lowly job as a worker. He had to carry large sheets of metal. In the days of the thirty-two eggs this would have been a trifle for him, a trifle boring maybe, but now it was worse than labor camp. He came home exhausted every evening and less than usual imbibing did the trick. A year into his new work, all fantasies about machines now in a hazy distant past, all interest in anything technical now dead, while carrying a large sheet of metal Cary was run over by a speeding car. It was a high Party official, late for dinner with his mistress ordering his chauffeur to step on the gas when this ghost of an engineer carrying his sheet of metal ignored the honking and instead of jumping to the side of the factory road, stayed his course.

Cary did not die as yet. A cranial fracture, seven fractured ribs and internal bleeding did not kill him. After a six-month hospital stay and a lecture about his politically reactionary attitudes he was sent home. Cary himself did the final job with a bottle.

With Cary out of the picture, the comrade Gheorghe Bucea had Viorica forcibly taken away from her mother and the countess was sent for a second stint in the labor camps.

By now, Ceauşescu, the "great leader," was ruling the country. On the other hand, I was doing my mathematics in the comfort of an American university. I got married, not to a countess, but in America that allegedly does not matter. I often talked to my wife about Cary. As a German, he could have left shortly after me, and he most likely did leave, I thought. By now he was probably the star engineer at Brown-Bovery at Siemens or at some other such corporation. If only we could find him. I tried, not surprisingly without success. After all these years I resolved that this past had become entirely disconnected from my present and as such was best severed from it. I dealt, as it were, with a truncated self in which there was no place for parasites, for engineers, for countesses. It was clear that I would never see any of these people again, never even see any of the places where we struggled, where we loved, where we hoped.

But then came the 1989 Revolution and suddenly Romania was on the map again. I was hesitant, should I go? Have things really changed? They did not abolish the Securitate after all, they only changed its name. But then, out of the blue, I got a pair of invitations to lecture there on my work and to attend a class reunion. I just couldn't pass up this opportunity.

So, there I was in 1992 in Timişoara . The buildings were all painted in beautiful hues of yellow, green, some even red and blue. The city was offering itself to tourists. There was only one condition, you weren't supposed to enter the buildings or notice the peeling paint, the plaster under it had not been repaired. They needn't have worried. The tourists stayed away.

I went to the reunion. It was awful. All those people I last saw thirty-five years ago were there, fat, bald, full of wrinkles, hard of hearing, limping, panting. What was I doing here? They all kissed me, I reciprocated, what else could I do? I immediately inquired about Cary. The moment I so much as mentioned his name, people pulled away. The only thing

I understood was that Cary "was no longer with us." Some blurted out Renée 's name? Renée , how could that be? She had been, or at least might have been, my girl. But how can you feel betrayed by a dead man, let alone feel anger?

As the kiss-and-get-reacquainted feast went on, I noticed a dark woman in the crowd, accompanying a fat bald old man. The fat bald old man had been a former classmate of mine when he was thinner and hairier. But I seemed to recollect the dark woman following him. I walked up to her and pretended she had also been a classmate. She had not, but she knew full well who I was, she was Flavia, Renée's student-days friend. It is from her I finally got the story straight. We missed the Rector's welcoming address, and the Dean's. We missed the keynote address by our former transformers professor, a decent man who finally at the age of seventy had discovered Kant and now wanted to convey his "usefulness" to "post-Marxist" Romania.

It was worth missing all this for I now finally got to know all about Cary and Renée. I learned that the second time around in labor camp she met Ivan Weiss. They got married. They worked in a coal mine under the most primitive conditions, not even ethylene lamps, a wonder they survived. They were now living in Arad and I resolved to visit them on the way out of the country. Flavia would let them know. We went back into the main hall where all speakers having had the floor, business was now proceeding on "updating" each other in alphabetical order on the past thirty-five years. The less they had to say, the longer people took to say it. Thus over twenty minutes were necessary to let us know that after having held five jobs over these years, Gelu Luca was now starting a pottery store, with capital whose origins remained unexplained, but for his past activities as a *Securitate* informer.

There were also tales sad and desperate in their own way. Not having been able to work as a woman engineer, Eufrosina Georgescu took another five years to study singing and made it to the Bucharest Opera chorus whence she retired at the age of fifty, now devoting herself to her only grandchild, orphaned when during a back-alley abortion his mother's uterus perforated. When we reached the H's, the university official in charge of reading the roster called out the name of Cornelius Hand and then loudly proclaimed "deceased," and started reading the next name, Sylvia Her . . . I got up at this point and barely mastering my emotion, I started, "If there was one engineering genius among us it was unquestionably Cary. I *understood* electrical machines; he *lived* them. I am devastated to learn about his death. It appears that his passion for Diesel-electrics combined with a misplaced loyalty to the machine factory here, literally wrecked his life." I sat down, hands still shaking and my body sweating profusely.

At this point Mr. Comrade Bucea got up and fixing his eyes on mine started, "Cary's loyalty to the machine factory was far from misplaced. He tried to make a contribution to the common good of the working class and at the same time make a living for himself and his wife." He was talking like the Party Secretary of old. I let it pass. I was not going to engage in polemics. That's not what American professors are meant to do in Dracula country.

So the roster reading went on: Sylvia Herlea, then came the I's, the J's ..... That same evening we all went for a "collegial dinner" to the student cafeteria. When I arrived, my former classmates were sitting on wooden benches alongside long tables. Suddenly from one of the benches I hear my last name being called and followed by the authoritative command, "Sit down here." It was Bucea. Knowing full well who I was dealing with and that the last dissonant chord had not yet been resolved, I sat down as commanded. Bucea, not one to waste a moment, went on, "Listen, I want you to promise me now, that you will agree with the remark which I am about to make." Four other overweight men, three bald, were sitting next to Bucea and now fixed their stares on me like spectators at a tennis match.

Warned I was, so I responded in kind, "You know Bucea, this is the most idiotic request I have had in quite some time. If you make a reasonable remark, why would I not agree with you? But if you treat me to some nonsense, how can you expect me to agree?" He was stunned at this "impertinence." While he was catching his breath, I went on: "It appears, both from this request and from your Cary-tirade this morning, that you have missed a beat somewhere. In the old days, when you were a Party bigwig and I was a Jew in bad standing, you often called my name and made remarks prefaced by the same request for me to agree beforehand. Now, try to recall, I always agreed with you. You knew it and I knew it that my disagreeing ever so slightly with whatever nonsense you had to say, would have given you the excuse to send me to a forced labor camp or to jail or wherever. But now, you might be surprised to learn, you couldn't send me to a forced labor camp or jail even if you tried. Now let's hear your 'remark.'"

"I don't have to make my remark, you made that unnecessary." I guess he wanted to find out whether I remembered who he was. I did! At that moment a waiter came to refill our beers and the four fellows by Bucea's side all cheered me, none cheered Bucea, he just gulped his beer down, as if I had parched him on the inside. This reunion was far from a pleasure for any of us.

The next day, I was leaving and had myself driven to Arad directly to Ivan Weiss and Renée 's place. It was four in the afternoon when I got there. Renée was there alone. I had a shock. She was no longer *my* countess, or anybody else's for that matter. Her posture was stunted, her hair was thin and gray, wrinkles lined the face where marble-toned skin had stretched. Gone was the elegance, gone the nobility. Left over were those blue eyes still radiating intelligence and now a sort of resignation. She stared at me as I must have been staring at her. We kissed on the cheeks. I embraced her again and she gently freed herself. "So nice to see you, so nice . . ." She sat down at a shabby round dining table covered with a red nylon "cloth" and began howling.

"Are you happy or unhappy?" I asked.

"Both," she replied as if that should have been obvious to me. "You don't know what I went through, you won't even understand it if I tell you, I'm afraid."

"I know, I know."

"No, you don't. Flavia may have told you this and that, but I have never been happy, not for a day. You know I married Cary." I nodded. "But he was not for me and now I have Ivan. You know where I used to stand on that. You know. Could *we* have been happy?"

"Not here, only had you followed me abroad."

"To live as an aristocrat in France, like *mon Papa* . . . And worst of all, the time is gone, it has been wasted. . . . There's nothing, literally nothing I can show for it. I am an old woman, I am the *Pique Dame*. I have no future and a very confused past. I wish I even didn't have this past. I wish I was young."

"That wish is universal." At this point I wanted to cheer her up and told her about my encounter with Bucea. She was not impressed.

"The 'courage' of Americans leaves me cold. Besides, isn't it a bit late to take on that bastard?"

"It is never too late."

"Oh, but I say it is. The son of a bitch raped me and then stole my daughter. He brought her up as if I did not exist. I wasn't even allowed to see her. But you know, after the revolution, they had to sacrifice a few of their own. Oh, they still all live in comfort, but at least some of them got *exposed*. You know what happened to him?" When I signaled that I didn't, she went on. "The truth about Viorica came out. It came out that I was alive. It came out that he raped me and Viorica overdosed the next day. It hurt, but if you ask me, it didn't hurt as badly as I thought it would. I had seen that child only for one year. Otherwise I had only fantasies to go by, like women who put illegitimate children up for adoption, or go for an abortion. It did not hurt, I am ashamed to admit. But *he* was devastated, he finally lost something precious. And all the Securitate, or whatever they call themselves now, could not put Viorica back together for him. You see, every story has two sides. Do you really think he cares about what you say? All he has left is the bottle, like Cary, and they say he is into it all the way by now. Ivan always wanted to 'implement freedom' in Romania. He used to say 'Communism has to go,' remember? And he was right. Communism is gone now, but implementing .... 'freedom' ...*here* . . come on . . ."

THE LOVE LIFE OF A JEWISH GARY COOPER

"I did it to hurt him, no question about that. For Béla I was a whore. He went as far as saying it to my face. Whore? All right, whore I'll give you. So I went to his buddy Philippe Baum's lab at the university and I knew Philippe's kink, the rest was easy. I had heard Philippe's story a hundred times, if I heard it once. I heard Béla tell it, I heard Philippe tell it to Béla, I heard faculty wives giggle about it. Philippe could only have sex if danger was involved. His entire sex life unfolded in his lab, where with doors unlocked he would have women perform acts on him minutes before the arrival of the students. That was it. I don't know how he got this way, I have my ideas on the subject, but to tell the truth I don't give a damn. For me Philippe was but a tool to give Béla his comeuppance.

And did it ever work! Just as Philippe started panting in the throes of his pleasure, the door opened and in walked Béla with the dean's wife just as I knew they would. Béla rushed at us, pulled me up by my shoulders, my teeth almost did to poor Philippe what men fear most, and then and there Béla hit me across my right cheek with a ferocity I had never suspected in him. I hated him that moment, I loved him at the same time. The dean's wife walked over and tried to comfort me, while shooing my husband away. That was it. We split up and I saw him one more time, he behaved the way I should have realized he would behave, but I always underestimate the meanness of men. That is why I am still rotting in this God-awful city at the edge of Transylvania, while my ex-husband and his buddy are sipping lemonade in some Tel-Aviv café or other. There is no justice. There never was."

———————

"If you ask me, Klári is a whore. I should have stayed away from her. I still can't understand how she got me to marry her. She bedded every blade of grass in town. My dean, she fucked my fucking dean, of all people! It must be that foul Transylvanian town, Arad, heavy, pretentious, dirty. The Hungarians let it rot right there on the shores of the muddy Maros. The Romanians, when they got it back after the Second World War, decided to make it into the one thing it was never meant to be, a cultural center. They created a university there. But then *you* try and find a Romanian who knows any chemistry and is willing to leave Bucharest to teach Hungarians in Arad. So they staffed the place with people in trouble, political trouble. The professor had been in the Iron Guard during the war and he was best relegated to some inconspicuous position. He was a first rate chemist and a decent guy where I was concerned. Maybe he learned something from his past, maybe he got chastened, or maybe he was just playacting, but I would be less than honest, were I to complain on his account. With me he was a gentleman. And who would be his assistants, but two Jews from Lugos, my buddy Philippe Baum and I.

"There was nothing to do in Fifties Arad. Go to the Russian movies, the one about Stakhanov exceeding his norm, or Michurin deflowering his flowers, or Popov inventing his radio? Read the newspapers and learn about the cow that gave more milk or the bull that got her with calf? Listen to the radio? No, all you could do was work and fuck. I worked with Philippe on a new family of polymers with possible industrial applications and this kept us busy during the day. After work I ran home and mounted Klári right there in the kitchen. She would protest, but if you ask me, she loved it.

"As to Philippe, I guess I should have paid more attention to his numerous recitations of woe. He did get a rough deal, no doubt about that. I guess it all started with that ill-fated engagement to Eva Vincze, the year the war ended, before the communist takeover. I was there, all of Lugos Jewry was invited at the Vincze villa on the bank of the Temes. They made a mighty handsome couple. Philippe had the good looks of a Jewish Gary Cooper and he had brains too. The guests had started indulging in the delicious buffet laid out by the bride's family and the French champagne purchased in Temesvár, some forty miles away. The toasts were about to start. The rabbi wanted the couple to step on the podium specially erected for the occasion. For a while the tall groom stood on it by himself, somewhat ill at ease, while the rabbi bid him to be patient 'You know women, they're always late, there's nothing to be done about it' and he was partially right. There *was* nothing, *absolutely* nothing, to be done about it. The bride had disappeared. They looked for her in the living quarters, in bathrooms, on the street, everywhere. Guests were nervously giggling at first, then they relaxed and started laughing. In the end the rabbi asked Philippe to step down from the podium. The Jewish Gary Cooper did so and clumsily tripped falling on his face like a Jewish Cary Grant. Big waves of roaring laughter now washed over the assembled guests as a dazed Philippe limped out of the room. Eva Vincze had eloped with Andris Weisz, with that jerk. Some start!

"During our student days in Bucharest, Philippe, equipped with *Ola Gummi* brand condoms was a regular at the brothel on the Chaussée. That was the full extent of his love life, not a single date, not one kiss. There were girls aplenty and they loved Philippe, but he had no interest in them, none whatsoever. That Vincze girl sure did a number on him.

"In Arad Klári and I managed to get a small walkup in an old apartment building from Austro-Hungarian days. As a bachelor, all that Philippe could manage was a room in the apartment of Katalin Szombathelyi a married woman with a three year old son, whose husband was in a labor camp for political reasons.

"Strapped for money, Katalin Szombathelyi offered Philippe room and board, she was a fine cook. Slowly Philippe took over as man of the house. They dined together, then put the little boy to bed and the long provincial winter evenings were spent by the tall green tile stove chatting, anyway at first. Katalin, a striking woman, a Hungarian Ingrid Bergman, put the Jewish Gary Cooper at ease and for the first time since the Lugos elopement he started talking about his utter devastation at the hands of his fiancée. No one had eloped at the Szombathelyi engagement or at the wedding which followed it, but a by no means lesser devastation was just as intensely visited on that married couple. Jancsi Szombathelyi, the groom, was a loudmouth and a womanizer. The latter devastated his wife, the former landed him in labor camp.

"Before long Philippe started making love to Katalin Szombathelyi. For the first time in his life the Jewish Gary Cooper was in love. They used to come over to our place and they looked happy, truly happy. But looks can be deceiving. The woman could not well divorce her husband while he was laboring in a camp, but Ingrid promised Gary she'd ask for a divorce from her Paul Henreid as soon as he came home.

"The Paul Henreids of the world always manage to survive and return, that's how they are typecast. Jancsi Szombathelyi was building the canal which was to connect the Danube before it forms its delta to the Black Sea. The fete was to be achieved by slave labor. They dug and dug the tract of the canal, but when time came to let the water in, the communists chickened out. The engineers were unanimous, you let the water in and with all due respect to Marx, Engels, Lenin *and* Stalin, all of Dobrogea, a good ten percent of the country would be flooded. Now they could blame that on some imperialist conspiracy, but at least those in power would know the truth and they could use it against each other in their Byzantine games. They opted for abandoning the project and sent the slaves home.

"Back in Arad, Jancsi Szombathelyi correctly assessed the situation: while he was away someone had been sleeping in his bed. That much he had expected. No one would cast Ingrid Bergman as the Holy Virgin. What irked Jancsi Szombathelyi was not the fact that in his absence a man had been fucking his wife, but the equally true fact that a handsome Jew had been at it. Jancsi demanded that his rival leave the apartment immediately, or else he vowed to 'kill the bastard'. A tearful Katalin appeared in Philippe's room and suddenly demoted him from Jewish Gary Cooper to Jewish Humphrey Bogart. She sent him packing with no more than a 'We'll always have Arad.'

What do Humphrey Bogarts do when their Ingrid Bergmans stay with their Paul Henreids? They go to their Claude Rains. Middle in the night Philippe showed up at my place. I sat up with him through the night. It wasn't 'the beginning of a beautiful friendship', Philippe and I were buddies since our Lugos childhood days. Moreover, a small detail, not important as yet, but with serious consequences yet to come, I was a married man, main difference between Claude Rains and me. Anyway, I talked and talked to Philippe the whole night. He wanted to kill himself, go to the lab and swallow cyanide. I talked him out of it and the result? Henceforth he could only have sex if danger was involved, if a sudden and possibly violent termination of the act appeared imminent. Much good did it do me, but I do not hold Philippe a grudge, had it not been him, Klári would have come up with someone else, she had no problems in this respect. I got what I had coming for marrying that whore. There is no justice. There never was."

"My best friend Béla Kelemen saved my life. I was about to end it all over what? Over a broad for laughing out loud. Now I know better, all I want is my cock sucked, no questions asked. For years it took an element of danger to get me going, but that has ended with that horrible business with Klári, some bitch, she staged that whole situation to drive a wedge between Béla and me. Fortunately he came to see reason and here in Israel we are still friends and still work together and now the field has been leveled, we're both unmarried. I have no trouble getting women, I bring them home, bed them, have them suck me off a couple of times and then I go to sleep. The ideal woman, as far as I am concerned is the one who is gone by the time I wake up. If she steels a sock or some money, I don't care, I have nothing of value in the house, just as long as I don't have to deal with the bitch when I get up.

My friend Béla isn't all that different, come to think. After he caught Klári in my lab he threw her out of his place, he did the right thing if you ask me. But of course she showed up a month later begging him to take her back. He said sure, all is fine and forgotten, took her in and fucked the daylights out of her. Next morning the movers showed up to take his furniture to a new place, he had to get out of this apartment, it reminded him of so many things he now wanted to forget. Klári thought this was an excellent idea.

'Where are we moving?' she asked.

'*I* am moving, you can stay if they'll let you, you whore.' That's Béla from Lugos for you, Béla Lugosi as we used to call him. He resented it, especially after he moved to Arad which *is* in Transylvania. "Leave me be with all that vampire crap" he would protest.

81

"When I got my papers to go to Israel, I called my former landlady, I owed her that much I thought. Her husband that Jew-hating son of a bitch was in Kolozsvár visiting his ailing mother. She came over to my place. Don't get me wrong, we did *not* make love. I wanted her to come with me. She started crying, she still loved me she claimed, but going to Israel was out of the question. Jancsi would never allow his son to become a citizen of 'Jew-country' as he called it and without the boy she would never come either.

'Do you want me to stay?' I asked her. She let go of a bitter bout of crying, but the upshot was *no,* she did not want me to stay either. Then what was all this crying about? Women have a need to be perceived as self-sacrificing, anyway those that don't have the need to sacrifice others. In either case sacrifice is central to their existence. Maybe that is because they give life and then feel they can deny it as well. Men can be cruel, no doubt, but we mostly predicate our lives on a live-and-let-live philosophy, none of this human sacrifice business. We may hail from Lugos and live in Transylvania, but that doesn't make us vampires. We believe in reason and justice, but if you hail from Lugos and have lived in Transylvania, you know there is no justice, there never was."

———————

"They took my husband to the Danube Canal and I was left alone to fend for myself and my little boy. A man moved in and from what he paid me for room and board we could subsist. He was a handsome fellow, a Jew, he was circumcised, he became my lover. His fiancée had eloped with another man and he had become the laughing stock of Lugos, his home town. I felt for him the way a woman feels for a young boy, very naïve, very needy, very attached. There was a security, a predictability to living with him. I liked that. He wanted to marry me, but I had a ready excuse, I was already married and I couldn't possibly walk out on Jancsi while he was at the Canal.

This all could have lasted for many more years, but then they sent Jancsi home and it all came to a boil. Jancsi was furious that I had taken up with a Jew. I told him I would never have married the guy, but that wasn't enough for my husband. 'What kind of an example were you setting for our boy, you might as well have had him circumcised.' He demanded I break up with Philippe. That was the easy part. I shed some tears, that always works with men, it gives them a sense of achievement. They either want you to tell them they are making you happy, or to shed tears if you cannot partake in the happiness they have in store for you. It makes them feel powerful, I guess.

But now to the ugly part. To 'punish' me, Jancsi started openly bringing women to the house and making love to them even within earshot of me and the boy. To the boy he justified it all as 'your mother is a Jew-lover, for her I have too much skin' and then he would maliciously burst out in laughter. After Philippe left for Israel, Jancsi divorced me, kept the boy and turned him against me. I had no visitation rights and had to watch my son being turned into a thug. That was not difficult under communism. By then Jancsi, to get his peace, had turned into a Securitate informer and my son became an outright scumbag, there is no other word for it. Egged on by his father he brought three Gypsy boys in front of my window and had them taunt me about my Jewish lover. I became the laughing stock of the housing project and ended up having to move away from Arad. I now live in Temesvár.

Should I have stayed with Philippe? Gone with him to Jew-country? Have him stay and protect me? He couldn't have protected me anyway, and those Gypsy taunts would have been all the more accurate.

"I am now starting life from scratch, away from everything I knew and have lived for before. I am not the youngest anymore. My God, what have I come to?

"I ran into Klári the other day, she came to Temesvár to see a play. We went to the bank of the river and sat down in the grass. It was nice seeing someone from my former life. She tells me Philippe and Béla are still busy with their polymers at some research institute in Tel-Aviv for a change. Neither of them got married. We laughed. After they got to know the Hungarian woman, neither of them could find happiness with those Middle-Eastern amazons. Then Klári shared with me a fantasy of hers, she wished the Arabs would invade Israel and drive the Jews into the sea. I nodded, I have had the same fantasy. But it will never happen. It's not their destiny and destiny is all there is, all there ever was.

BEYOND RAMEAU

"The great Stalin is the father of all children in the world" proclaimed the worn poster in the tram stop, but Timişoara fathers knew better: they politely ignored the mustachioed dictator's claim, and went about their usual business of showering love on daughters and putting down sons as if they were their very own.

So, on a crisp November Sunday morning Ödön Auscher plopped himself in the center of the Philharmonic's lobby. From there he could survey the flow of people rushing to the coat checks. He could selectively wave to a friend here, to an acquaintance there, and remind them that this was his day. It was the regular Sunday morning concert of the Timişoara Philharmonic and Anna, Ödön's daughter, was to be the piano soloist. In Ödön's book the twelve-year-old Anna rated a comparison with "Cortot at the same stage of his career,"

The nerve-racking sound of the big bell, announced to latecomers it was time to run, the small dark-skinned conductor was about to raise his baton. Ödön took his place in the left proscenium box. For him, the main virtue of the first piece was its brevity. Barely had the applause following it died down, than the small conductor and his soloist made their appearance to a universal "aaahhh" sound in the hall.

In her black dress, her thick dark hair flowing, Anna cut a dramatic figure as she sat down at the piano and went through the traditional ritual of pianists optimizing the position of their behinds. Were it not for her diminutive figure, one would have expected her to play Chopin, Grieg, or Tchaikovsky. Instead, the orchestra started and then the warm, tender tones of the piano blended in the reverie of a Mozart Concerto. The dangerous cadenzas were negotiated with the aplomb and virtuosity of a much more mature artist. The event was a resounding success.

Anna became a once-a-year regular at the Philharmonic concerts until, in 1955, at the age of seventeen, she was dispatched to the Conservatory in Bucharest. She was Ödön's great hope. In his otherwise uneventful life he saw himself as having sired Timişoara's answer, if not to Alfred Cortot, well, then, to Dinu Lipatti. This is not to imply that the relationship between Ödön and his daughter was limited to the push of the ambitious father. True, on rare occasions Ödön did resort to physical punishment, yet even this was administered with a measure of love, and in spite of the physical pain inflicted, unquestioningly accepted by Anna. On the whole, Ödön simply doted on his daughter. He could sit for hours listening to her practice, much to Anna's delight.

After completing her scales, chords, and other finger exercises, she would pull out one of Ödön's favorite composers, Schumann, Chopin, or curiously enough, Rameau. At her age she had trouble with the more fiery pieces of the romantic repertory, what with her small frame and gentle hands — she could barely squeeze out an octave here and there — but Rameau suited her. Baroque, yes, but Rameau knew the grand line and even in his rococo times missed by very little being the first romantic.

Ödön had wanted to buy Anna a *cemballo* or a *clavecin*, but in Stalinist Romania all a Jew could hope for was to somehow get out to Israel, and this was hardly the time to buy period instruments. So Anna played Rameau on the old family Bösendorfer on which he sounded grand, grander than in his natural habitat.

After such a session, father and daughter would adjourn to the kitchen and make small talk to Clara, the tiny matriarch preparing their meal. Ödön would stand behind Anna, her head fit snugly under his chin, which he liked to rest on the partition of her rich hair. His warm brown eyes were radiating satisfaction and a kind of transfiguration called forth by love. Below, the large dark eyes of his daughter were sending a message of inner peace, of duty accomplished, but not without a tinge of malaise, of an insecurity hard to conceal. What did the future hold?

There is a physical side to being a piano virtuoso, a forceful, resilient body and large hands are the prerequisites *sine qua non*. But Anna was developing into a carbon copy of Clara, the petite woman with filigree hands.

For now, perfectly presented Rameau and Mozart with a worthy phrasing would earn her the appreciation of the audience. But inevitably there comes a point where a Beethoven is struggling to emerge. Every young pianist reaches this point, and it is here that the men are separated from the boys, or — as in this case — the woman from the girl. For Anna this point was reached when she moved to Bucharest, where Ödön got her a nice room with kitchen privileges three blocks from the Conservatory.

With her credentials, Anna was auditioned the very first week by the *grande-dame*, Florica Muzicescu, Lipatti's legendary teacher. She played Rameau and Mozart, but Madame Muzicescu asked for Schumann. Anna obliged, but the old lady was not impressed. "Soul is necessary but not sufficient. *Technique, physique, mademoiselle*," was the summary judgment with which she dismissed Anna. "Anti-Semitism" was Ödön's lapidary answer to this affront. So Anna was assigned to one of the other still high-ranking teachers at the conservatory. But then, by the end of her second year, she had been irrevocably dumped from the pack of highly promising students, and it had been made clear to her that she had better consider the alternatives: piano teacher, coach, chamber music, rehearsal pianist, high school music teacher. At this point Anna wired home that she was going blind. What with Beethoven deaf, Ödön rushed down to Bucharest in a Wagon-Lit, and brought Anna home.

A visit to Dr. Pohr, the old eye-specialist by the Catholic Cathedral established that blindness was not the problem, Anna but needed stronger eyeglasses. With Cortot, Lipatti ever further out of reach, Ödön did not relent, "So you're going to specialize in Rameau, and early Mozart. Let the Goyim do the romantics", the hand size was not mentioned. Anna desperately tried to convey to her father that it was over, but he could not and would not accept that as a fact. Anna was to "bring back Rameau" and thereby give a sense to his own life.

Next fall, with Rameau carefully tied around her neck, she was back in Bucharest. While guilt and routine still had her practicing eight hours a day in the dingy little cubicles at the Conservatory, she for the first time joined a chamber music group. She started accompanying tenors and baritones who in turn started accompanying her to her room. By the middle of her last year she had her first abortion and had moved in with a blond percussionist. Rumors about these goings-on reached Timișoara. Ödön discounted them as malicious. On the other hand,

Clara and the other women in the family decided to marry Anna off. It was a real conspiracy.

Before the Communist takeover Ödön had been a wealthy industrialist, but his factory had been nationalized and his gold holdings confiscated by Romania's new rulers. Evicted from the villa on the factory grounds, the Auschers were ever since making do with a two-room-plus-kitchen apartment in what was more or less a slum. The Bösendorfer grand took up much of one of the rooms, the rest was one big dormitory with a dining table added. Clara's dressing table, disconnected from its mirror, doubled as a bridge table and was extensively used by the distraught remnants of the Jewish bourgeoisie in their attempt to recapture the days past. It was over a hand of bridge that the match was made.

Ivan Schwarz, the son of a Oradea physician, was studying chemical engineering at the Timişoara Polytechnic. A true mama's boy, he did not have powerful enough instincts to attend to his hideous acne, whether in the company of a woman, or by himself. A real devotee of classical music, he was a technically proficient, if otherwise uninspired, piano player. His mother fell for the past grandeur embodied in the Bösendorfer purchased years earlier at full price from a dealer, rather than as a bargain from some starving former owner. With her seal of approval, it took but one viewing of pubescent Anna's portrait — painted the year they lost the factory — to convince Ivan that he had found a bride. Anna was summoned from Bucharest, but put up rebellious opposition with Ödön 's adoring support.

On the third day after Anna's return, Clara, who had suddenly lost a lot of weight, was diagnosed with terminal cancer and given nine months at the utmost. Under the circumstances her will prevailed and a wedding date was, as it turned out, well chosen. The weather was auspicious, it was in early May, everything was in bloom, Clara was still in passable shape, and the future seemed promising. Giving away his beloved daughter, his petite Rameau expert, Ödön had that same proud look with which he had surveyed the crowds on the occasion of Anna's Philharmonic debut. After all, he knew she had not been written entirely out of his life. This sweaty-palmed youngster with the Chaplinesque walk was but a minor imposition on the very special, if as of late limited, relationship he had with his daughter.

The Bucharest rumors notwithstanding, as far as Ödön was concerned, Anna only too well deserved the bridal white, she was still his little virgin.

Precisely on this account, li'l Chaplin held so weak a threat for the loving father. Making love to such a boy would be a gentle, controlled business, she would still be qualified to play Rameau and early Mozart. No passions would be aroused that might call forth Beethoven.

He should have known better, for in the Synagogue at Anna's request a Rameau introduction was followed up with an organ rendition of the *Liebestod* from *Tristan und Isolde*. A shudder went through the congregation. If Wagner in a Jewish house of prayer was not bad enough, why precisely the *Liebestod* on this balmy spring afternoon on which a marriage was to be performed. A visibly disturbed Ödön brushed it off as the effect of Conservatory training. However, the Mendelssohn march soon sounded and the ladies sighed with relief when it was all over.

A big bash, with Anna's childhood friends in the dark Bösendorfer room was tight on space but rich on food and emotion. People were sitting on and under the concert grand, dancing around it, while feasting on goose *pâté*, smoked ham, Russian salad, homemade *foie gras* —hereabouts force fed geese could be cheaply purchased live in the market place— *icra*, the roe of carp, and *Dobos*, *Punch*, and Hazelnut tortes, along with fine white wine from Recaş. The groom's well-to-do family paid for the event, the Auschers made it feel like the good old days.

Around midnight the newlyweds took the last tram for the city center, where a room at the Carlton Hotel was awaiting them. Their departure was hardly noticed by the well boozed-up crowd that danced into the wee hours and only left after the customary pungent *sauerkraut* broth with fresh sour cream and well-dried Hungarian *kolbász* was served to fortify them for the walk home.

In June Anna took her final examinations at the Conservatory and the boy, his acne finally under some control, graduated from the Polytechnic. Judiciously placed bribes, paid for by Ivan's father, procured them jobs in Cluj. An old cultural center, it sported two opera houses and a symphony orchestra, and Anna was employed as rehearsal pianist with the symphony chorus, whereas Ivan was working in an all-blue aniline dye factory.

They were installed in a Cluj apartment by early September. Later that month Clara had to be hospitalized. Anna, on emergency leave, was sitting with Ödön at her bedside, father and daughter, hand in hand, silently by the heavily sedated mother-wife who had never penetrated the mysteries of their unique relationship. Little was said, but by the time Clara was resting in peace in the old section of the Jewish cemetery, more than just one side of a closely-knit family triangle had been removed. No place was left for Rameau or early Mozart.

A bereaved Ödön visited the young couple twice during the fall. Blue Boy was an unexpected major intrusion in the father-daughter relation, a very major intrusion indeed. On the second visit he alone entertained Ödön, while Anna could spare but one evening from the demanding rehearsals for Beethoven's Ninth.

Ödön had come to discuss emigration to Israel. With Stalin's mummy resting in the mausoleum for some years now, the Romanian communist government had decided to restart Jewish emigration to Israel, as a highly profitable business venture. American Jewish charities were paying the going per-head rate for every Jew leaving the country. This rate was being continuously adjusted not unlike the price of a stock, based on a supply and demand type formula. To keep up appearances, the official reason for this emigration was given as family reunification. In other words, Jews were not leaving communist Romania, God forbid, nor were they going to "imperialist" Israel, perish the thought, they were simply rejoining their loved ones somewhere abroad. Whole families were being granted exit visas as units. It was of essence to decide which family unit one applied to emigrate with. The upshot of Ödön 's visit to Anna and Ivan was an agreement that the young couple would apply to emigrate with the Schwarz family unit. This seemed to fit everyone's needs. Just before he left, Ödön asked Anna to play his favorite Rameau Suite, a kind of farewell, to something.

That July, emigration was imminent and neither Blue Boy nor his rehearsal pianist wife could concentrate on their work. This did not mean that they concentrated on their marriage — the acne was as bad as ever. On a hot Wednesday, on account of materiel shortages, the engineer came home earlier than usual. He took the squeaky elevator to the third floor apartment and to his surprise found three French horns in the small hall. He crossed the kitchen and opened the back door to the bedroom. In it Anna was rapturously submitting to one horn player, with two more impatiently awaiting their turn in the open door to the living room. The atmosphere was charged enough that this intrusion passed unobserved. Ivan left the house in a daze and headed for the railway station.

That same evening in Oradea, he broke down in his mother's arms and she immediately notified Ödön. The contract had been violated. The wedding expenses, the bribes, the Cluj apartment had all been paid for, and yet the Rameau-playing angel from that early portrait was messing around not with one or two but with three men, horn-players to boot. Ödön 's fury was aroused, though for a moment, just a moment, his brown eyes flickered with irony. He had always likened the use of the portrait in the wooing of Wet-Palms to the Queen of the Night's wooing of Tamino with nothing more than her daughter's portrait in the *Magic Flute*. Now Figaro was taking over, he could hear the horns warning of female infidelity. But this was an affront to him too. So maybe those Bucharest stories were true. Ödön took the next train to Cluj. There he found an Anna who would have none of the "let's be reasonable"-s or "what kind of behavior is this?"-s. "Wake up Daddy, I am no longer playing Rameau."

Ivan had been reasonable, he had behaved like a gentleman. He had grabbed the phone from his mother, and, amidst all the threats and curses, managed to get across to Ödön that he would not sue for divorce until they reached Israel. Otherwise, were a divorce to be granted before they left, Anna would be stuck in Romania, ineligible for emigration for many years to come, hard to communicate with even by mail. Still, Anna wanted a divorce and she wanted it there and then. Ödön used all his sense of persuasion in vain.

She wanted out. They were at it for hours and were getting nowhere. In desperation, Ödön took hold of Anna, sat down on the bed, laid her across his knees and took off his leather belt. He belt-whipped his daughter for three full minutes. A fury of immense proportions had come over him and he was crying. Anna was silent except for an occasional painful sigh. It was Rameau's revenge, a romantic after all, the old fellow, real *Sturm und Drang*.

When it was all over, they rested. The exhausted father helped the young woman up, "Are you all right?" Anna nodded, she felt humiliated, more for him than for herself, but she also felt relieved, as if a great burden had been lifted from her shoulders. She went to the kitchen and shouted to her father, still numbly sitting on the bed of his shame, "Want a coffee?" Ödön got up and walked slowly into the kitchen. For the first time in his life he felt old. Slowly, but deliberately he walked up behind Anna and put his arm around her shoulder. They stood like that until the coffee started percolating, then silently sat at the table for a long while.

"All right," Anna broke the silence. "I'll wait till we get to Israel."

"Thank you" was the cryptic reply as Ödön reached for Anna's hand. He left that same evening. This was the last time they saw each other. Maybe they both knew it, maybe they both wanted it that way.

A month later Ödön got his emigration papers and left heavy-hearted with his eightyish mother-in-law. The night before, he called Anna one last time, she couldn't come and see them to the border on account of some important rehearsals. They talked about meeting soon in Israel, and assured each other that everything was forgotten and that they loved each other as before.

The day after Ödön disembarked in Haifa, Anna sued for divorce and obtained it well before her ex-spouse left for the Israeli aniline industry. When Ödön got the news — not from Anna, but orally from Ivan in Tel-Aviv — he had a coronary. Anna was granted an exit visa allowing her to attend the funeral. The Schwarz family generously offered to underwrite her round-trip, but she could not fit it into her schedule.

Years after her father's death, Anna, alone in her cold one-room Cluj apartment, sat down at the piano and on a sudden urge got out the score of Rameau's Suites. She started playing slowly, hesitantly at first. Then her fingers took off on their own and infused the music with a deep romantic sensibility, as never before. When she finished, she sat for a moment, as if hit by a special revelation, then sighed, frowned, and finally started smiling. She got up, picked up the score, held it for a moment and then with great urgency started tearing it up. When the whole score was in shreds, the words coming from a loudspeaker in the street suddenly registered in her consciousness "Long may you live our great leader Comrade Ceaușescu, we all are your grateful children."

THE THIRTEENTH CHAIR

A year after they nationalized the Blumenthal Brewery, the Romanian communist authorities decided to remodel the former owners' on-site residences into a large hall for workers' meetings. Despite the pervasive yeast odor, the Blumenthal brothers Dezsö and Pali had been living on the brewery's premises on the shore of Temesvár's Bega Canal. Their residence, a heavy building separated from the river canal by a row of tall poplars, contained two solid apartments, one for Dezsö, the elder brother and his large family, and a slightly smaller one for Pali, who with his daughter and son-in-law had been its last occupants.

The demolition work started on Pali's wing. Thick walls were being ripped out and the structure did not collapse as had been feared. This encouraged the party officials in charge, to complete the project as ordered by the regional committee. Just as they thought it was coming to a successful conclusion, they were faced with a big surprise. The last wall to be torn down, the thickest, had barely been opened, when instead of the expected interior structure to be taken apart brick by brick, they hit a layer of solid oak, which when axed open, poured forth a shower of gold coins, French Napoleons, Austrian coins bearing the likeness of His Royal and Imperial Majesty Franz Joseph, Swiss *vrenelis,* some ten thousand coins in all. The police and the *Securitate* were immediately alerted and it was ordered that this cache be delivered to the coffers of the Communist Party. The question of its provenance and legality came up naturally. One of the earliest laws enacted by the communists forbade the private ownership of precious metal coins and of any form of foreign currency. It specified that any individual holding such assets had to declare and surrender them to the state no later than one month after the law's enactment. This law had been violated, there was no doubt about that. The obvious violator was Dezsö Blumenthal in whose apartment the treasure lay buried. But it was common knowledge that Dezsö had been felled by a stroke a month after he had been evicted from his apartment. His sudden demise became more understandable with the discovery of the walled gold. Under interrogation, his son Bandi admitted knowledge of the existence of his father's hidden treasure, but claimed that his father had never shared any details about its size or location with him. According to Dezsö's son, the gold had been hidden in the Thirties to protect it from confiscation by the fascists who ruled the country then. It had apparently not been removed from its hiding place in the brief interim between fascism and communism, the only time when Jews could have used it with impunity. Bandi's place was ransacked by the authorities, just in case something lay hidden there, but, it appeared, the young man was speaking the truth.

The matter seemed to wind down, but then one *Securitate* captain asked a new question. This meeting hall was being carved out of two adjacent apartments formerly belonging to two brothers. One brother had a wall full of gold. How about the other brother? Clearly, all his walls had been torn down as well and none were found to contain any gold. But when of two brothers, partners in business, one bought a lot of gold, it stood to reason, so this captain suggested, that the other brother should also have acquired gold holdings. Did he declare them and then surrender them to the state, as the law required? The gold and currency surrender logs at City Hall showed that nothing of the sort had taken place. So where was Pali's gold? Unlike Dezsö, his brother Pali was alive and well, one more indication that he had not yet parted with his gold cache.

Without wasting any time, the *Securitate* descended on Pali, who was now living in one room of an apartment, which he shared with two young couples and a prostitute who plied her trade in her room. The *Securitate's* arrival around midnight caused quite a commotion, especially in the whore's room. Her trick panicked and started running away but in the end was picked up by the guard stationed on the street and arrested along with Pali. When it turned out that this trick was a party member in good standing, he was released and the agents could concentrate on the matter that brought them to the apartment in the first place.

Under his silver mane, Pali's smooth, pale, shiny face was as expressionless as ever. His understandable fear was betrayed only by the visible quiver of his purple lips. This subtle expression of terror was not lost on Captain Cojocaru, his interrogator, a specialist in the administration of fear. To utterly confuse Pali, so as to better pounce on him when he least expected it, Captain Cojocaru pretended to an interest in Pali's life story. He seemed to have many facts at his fingertips in a voluminous file. He was not parading these facts in front of the old man, but was asking questions to which he well knew the answers. Whatever answer Pali came up with in the middle of a sleepless night, the captain made more precise by fleshing it out with a significant, and fully accurate detail.

"What was your interest in the Blumenthal Brewery. Comrade?"

"My late brother Dezsö and I owned the brewery"

"which you inherited from your father, one David Blumenthal .... It says so here" and he pointed to the file. "Did you own equal shares of this family business?"

"No, my brother owned three quarters, I only owned one quarter"

"It says here, you sold him half your shares in 1910. Why?"

"I needed the money to pursue a career in the arts"

"Could you elaborate?"

"In 1910 I headed for Vienna, to study painting. Through a friend I got acquainted with Gustav Klimt who took me on as an assistant"

"Who is this Gustav ...?"

"He was a famous Austrian painter known for his portraits of women"

"What kind of women? Working class? Peasant?"

"Not really, mostly women from wealthy families"

"I understand, a painter of the bourgeoisie, I see, I see" at this the Captain jotted down some quick notes. "It says here that you married a certain Marianne Lieb there. What happened to this woman?"

"I wouldn't know, we got divorced a long time ago." The captain started laughing sarcastically. His dossier probably contained the juicy details of this divorce, which had been the talk of the town when it happened. Like all juicy gossip it made it into the files of the *Siguranța,* the prewar Royal security police, files the *Securitate* had inherited.

The elopement and subsequent divorce of Marianne Lieb had indeed been quite an item. She had met and married Pali in Vienna while he was Klimt's assistant, a position which appeared to be a major first step in Pali's artistic career. Yet, steps gain importance only if they form a path. Sadly for Pali no such path was being formed and two years later he returned to the shores of the Bega canal a better colorist, but alas not an artist. The man who brought Marianne Lieb to Temesvár was a deeply changed Pali. Though barely thirty, he was already a bitter old man. His lips were pursed in a chronic expression of pent-up rage, which every now and then partially relieved itself in the form of a sneer. He painted still, but knew the result was not by a long shot what he had wanted. In Vienna he had learned what a good work of art was meant to look like and he knew that his portraits — he painted exclusively portraits — missed the mark. As if to break with the past in as definitive a manner as possible, he decided to "Hungarize" his name to Etri and took to signing his portraits with his new initials PE. This Hungarization was also timely. It was 1914, the war had just broken out and no one could question an Etri's allegiance to the Hungarian fatherland. To top it all, he joined a Jewish Free Mason lodge, in the hope that this would benefit both his career and his standing in society.

By early 1915 Marianne bore Pali a daughter Clara. Though attended to by a nanny, three chambermaids and a cook, Marianne fell into a deep depression following the birth of her daughter. This went unnoticed by her Free Mason husband and this total neglect led Marianne close to the shores of suicide. Before landing though, she took on a new habit, taking long aimless strolls through this provincial city; she had read somewhere that such strolls invigorate the body and cheer up the mind. When returning from one of these strolls she saw a crowd in front of a house on the Haymarket. Intrigued, she walked up to it to see what the commotion was all about. An agitated bespectacled youngster was announcing that he had clearly heard a spy in the basement. With *"Der Feind hört mit!"* posters at every corner, a veritable spy hysteria had been whipped up in wartime Temesvár and the crowd was understandably excited to confront the living proof of enemy skullduggery. Suddenly an Austrian Captain — although located in Hungary, for historical reasons Temesvár had an Austrian garrison — stepped up and commanded the youth to take him to the basement door. The captain drew his saber and charged into the basement. Moments later he emerged smiling, holding a tabby kitten by its neck. He asked the youth "Is this the spy you heard?" The youngster's face visibly reddened and the crowd roared with laughter. Even Marianne couldn't resist the urge and was shaken by a healthy bout of laughter, the first such bout in months. It was at this very moment that the Austrian captain, noticed Marianne, clicked his heels, smiled, and saluted in her direction. Marianne acknowledged the greeting with a nod and a smile. Less than an hour later, in a quite seedy hotel Marianne was giving the captain that which her Free Mason had stopped taking from her. The captain was scheduled to return to Vienna three days later and in the event eloped with Marianne.

With his hopes for an artistic career completely dashed and now his young wife gone as well, Pali viewed life as a burden bravely to be carried as best he could, with some help from the Free Masons and precious little else by way of comfort or understanding. His brother was too absorbed in the beer business to bother about the quality of some painting or other, or the whereabouts of his sister-in-law for that matter. To his credit, Pali made a real effort to bring up little Clara. He showered her with gifts and gave her the best care and education money could buy. He kept this up until at age twenty Clara married Joska Klein, a lawyer, who then joined father and daughter in the apartment by the Bega Canal. The young woman's life revolved ever more definitely around her husband. Pali reverted to Free Masonry as the focus of his existence.

Already during the war Dezsö, who had the controlling interest in the brewery, thoroughly disapproved of Pali's change of name "Our money comes from Blumenthal beer and not some Etri beer" he repeatedly reproached Pali. He was about to be proven much more right than he had any reason to suspect, for the war soon came to an end and with it so did the Habsburg Empire. Temesvár was ceded to Romania and its name changed to Timişoara. Henceforth a Hungarian name was even more reviled than a Jewish one. Pali acceded to his brother's wish, went through a second name change and thereby restored his original family name.

"I see here that you changed your name twice" intoned Captain Cojocaru somewhat menacingly.

"So I did, but don't ask me why, I couldn't tell you"

"Most likely you were running from something" volunteered the captain and then sprang the question "incidentally where do you keep your gold?"

"I don't know what you are talking about" replied the Free Mason with all the insouciance he could muster. But the captain saw through this pose and in a much more severe tone repeated his question. When he still didn't get a straight answer, he very matter-of-factly spelled out to the former Blu-menthal Beer co-owner his predicament. Even when, with feigned reluc-tance, he started warning Pali that there were physical methods to extract the truth, he did not get the expected cooperation. He had seen this before, men willing to defy threats of violence, on the false assumption that their tormentor was bluffing. So he escalated his threat one notch. He pushed a button and a minute later two aides appeared at the door with two gray boxes. From the extensive wear on these two pieces of equipment, it was clear that they had received a lot of use. Blotches of dried blood were clearly visible on both boxes. With the detachment of a teacher about to give a lecture to a new student, the captain explained to Pali that one of the boxes was used for administering electric shocks to the scrotum, indicating by a gesture that Pali was expected to lower his pants and underwear. Then he went on to describe the other box into which the person being interrogated was to insert one hand and then withdraw it with one fingernail removed. If his cooperation did not improve, the process could be repeated up to a maximum of ten times if needed. The captain proudly explained that the machine was of such clever design that its handedness could be adjusted at will, thus doubling its capacity. This gruesome explanation given with a smile and in a friendly soft tone did the trick. When the captain suggested that Pali first insert his left hand for size, the Free Mason passed out. The captain exchanged knowing smiles with his aides, they must all have seen versions of this scene before. Smelling salts available in the office brought Pali back to consciousness and in answer to the interrogator's pregnant "so?" Pali started spilling the beans. Yes he also had gold holdings, just as the captain had guessed, but unlike his older brother, he did not bury his gold in the walls of his apartment, he hid it in the attic of the house in which his daughter Clara and her husband were renting two rooms.

Captain Cojocaru accompanied by three *Securitate* sergeants headed directly for that attic and at the exact spot indicated by the old man he found in a leather pouch one thousand gold coins, quite a bit fewer than in Dezső's wall-bound treasure, but still nothing to sneer at. The Securi-tate team arrested Clara and along with the gold brought her back to head-quarters. Here the captain staged a father-daughter confrontation, hoping to learn from their demeanor whether they were truthful or whether there was more hidden elsewhere. At the sight of his handcuffed daughter the old man squinted, then with an air of utter resignation lowered his head. An uneasy smile settled on Clara's mouth and stayed there for the rest of this confrontation. Years after having lost his wife to an Austrian army captain, Pali's relation with his daughter, his only remaining family, was being undone by a Romanian *Securitate* captain. After some further questioning it became clear to this officer that there was no more gold, so he told the old man he was free to go. Even in communist Romania people beyond a certain age had immunity from criminal prosecution for financial wrongdoing. By contrast, the captain announced, Clara would have to stand trial as an accomplice. It had been her legal duty to denounce her father and she had failed to do so. After fingerprinting Clara, the captain released her on bail.

Clara's trial took place one month later, her husband Joska was her attorney. She was sentenced to one year in jail. Pali did not come to court, nor did he ever visit his daughter in jail. He became ever more withdrawn and taciturn. With all the goings-on in the apartment in which his small room was located, Pali experienced an acute shortage of privacy. Not unlike Marianne, he took to roaming the streets by day. Invariably he'd end up along the Bega Canal and follow the water towards the outskirts of the city, to where the river proper started, wide, open, muddy. There were no bridges out there, but there was a hand-operated ferry. Pali would ferry himself to the other shore and stare back at the city. He could spend hours doing this. One week before Clara's release, while operating the ferry, Pali had a stroke. He lay motionless on the bottom of the ferry. Things were confused in his mind. The famous movie of one's life being unreeled in the last moment was a kind of slow motion picture in Pali's case. Marianne Lieb was floating fairy-like on the shimmering water. She was laughing and Pali couldn't tell whether she was having a good time or was just plain scornful. When sufficiently slowed down, laughter looses its character. Presently Clara joined her mother on the water, but she did not laugh, she just nervously produced the uneasy smile he had last seen on her face. Suddenly the two women donned ornate Klimtian dresses and posed ready to be painted, but he had neither the means nor the strength to capture their likenesses. From the city-side riverbank a captain in Napoleonic uniform approached in a slow-moving boat rowed by four young men in chains. In his mind Pali reached for the wafting silk of the women's garments, but it was all in vain. The captain, wrapped in a large gray flannel cape, with his back to Pali, suddenly stood over the old man's body. A slimy goo enveloped Pali and he no longer remembered how to breathe.

AH, THAT OCEANIC FEELING!

In the nineteenth century, Fyodor Mikhailovich Dostoyevski had faced a firing squad; they didn't fire at him. In the twentieth century I also faced a firing squad, and they didn't fire at me either. All resemblance ends there. To state but the obvious, Fyodor Mikhailovich was a rabid anti-Semite whilst I am a Jew, or staying still with the obvious, Dostoyevski never could have heard of Nikita Khrushchev, whereas I, in a perverse sense, owe my life to that bald communist's gullibility. And then there is this minor detail: I never wrote about crime and punishment. True, the firing squad was meant to punish me, but I had committed no crime, I never even owned an ax.

It all started on a rainy November afternoon in 1956. Cursed with a heredity that inexorably leads to shiny baldness, my Jewish mother had tried on me all the remedies then on the books and even some not yet released to the health-conscious public. One such word of mouth remedy had the prospective baldness victim soak his hair on six consecutive occasions in castor oil, and each time let the oil "absorb deeply" into the scalp for twenty-four hours. Given the nauseating smell and oily appearance of my head, I stayed home that November afternoon, did some homework and didn't get out of the house till the next morning, by which time the smell, though not the oily sheen, was gone, I had to go to classes at the Timişoara Polytechnic where I had started my fourth year. Barely had I reached the front entrance to my department, when it became clear that something very much out of the ordinary was afoot. Standing in the door and summarily waving us away was the dean himself, a tense black-haired man in his forties, who used such immense quantities of brilliantine, that his rich black hair looked as if though he as well, even without the prompting of a Jewish mother, had soaked it in castor oil. He wouldn't answer any questions, he just nervously kept waving us away until we got the idea and left. That this was political was obvious to us all. For days we had all been glued to Radio Budapest as we listened to the hour-by-hour developments in the Hungarian capital. Imre Nagy had taken over the government, Cardinal Mindszenthy had been freed from jail. It was possible! The hour of liberation had arrived! Not for nothing had General Eisenhower stated during the American Presidential campaign that, *as is,* he could do nothing, but if the peoples of the Soviet satellites were to install governments which *asked* for American help, he would not hesitate to come to their aid. With Hungary already out of Soviet orbit, Romania was clearly next to go. Finally something was happening and the dean at the front door was the herald of our liberation.

What do you do when a revolution is in the making and classes have been canceled? Obviously, you go out to Main Street, the *Corso,* and keep on top of events. I did just that with my friend Robby Telkes. We started what the French call *flâner,* walking aimlessly up and down that street. Barely ten minutes into this exercise, we were approached by a student who, with a distinct air of mystery, managed to whisper "at eleven, meeting in front of the Agronomic Institute" before quickly disappearing.

Robby and I rushed up to my place where we left our bags in order to proceed unencumbered to the meeting. My mother wised up and had me promise we wouldn't "get involved in anything". No, I replied, we would just watch from Robby's living room window, which looked out on the Agronomic Institute. Followed by her worried looks, we rushed out straight for the meeting. The last thing I heard as we ran, was her reminder "and be sure to come home by latest one o'clock, so you wash out the castor oil from your hair". "You have castor oil in your hair?" Robby roared with laughter "have you 'upset' your head?" I reprimanded him with a reproachful look, how could he talk about such trivia when we were about to march headlong into history, but he answered with a frown that clearly stated "look man, you aren't Marat as yet". We both cracked up, at nineteen you wish for drama, but are basically into laughing fate off.

In front of the Agronomic Institute we finally got a clear picture of what all the fuss was about. Apparently the previous afternoon a spontaneous meeting had been called in the big hall of the Polytechnic. Many students with scalps not soaked in castor oil attended, as did the president of the University and a high official from Bucharest. It was meant to be the kind of meeting to calm the troops, to keep them from doing something stupid, but it quickly got out of hand. The high official from Bucharest encouraged the students to say whatever they wanted without any fear of reprisals. Thereupon the students started expressing their sympathy for the Hungarians. Nobody had expected *that*. To hear Romanian students sing the praises of Hungarians is somewhat like Arabs swooning about the Jews, or vice versa. The high official then claimed he had intended the unusual freedom of speech to refer solely to academic matters and together with the president made a hasty exit from the hall. The vast majority of students got the idea and left in a hurry as well. A small group however stayed on and were busy writing a manifesto, but they didn't get very far. *Securitate* agents suddenly entered the hall and arrested the lot of them. A curfew was proclaimed and overnight another hundred students or so were picked up on the street. From the meeting at the Agronomic Institute we were going to march on the headquarters of the Communist Party to demand that all our classmates be freed, and while at it, that Romania be freed from Russian occupation.

Ah, that oceanic feeling that overcomes you when you lock step with some two thousand like-minded youngsters for what you deeply believe is a just cause. We left the yellow Agronomic Institute, crossed the main bridge over the river on our way to the yellow Communist Party building. We were just halfway, at the Orthodox Cathedral, when suddenly the nearby girls' dorm came in view. It had been sealed by the *Securitate*, and they wouldn't let anyone in or anyone out. The trapped girls came to their windows, by the hundreds and started shouting at the top of their lungs "Save us! Save us!" Imbued with oceanic feeling as we already were, the sight of these girls got our testosterone flowing. By God we were going to storm the dorm and carry these Sabine women with us. It never got that far, for as we made the detour from our march on the Party building and readied ourselves for storming the dorm, we were suddenly, out of the blue, surrounded by army troops with guns pointed at us. To be fully accurate, these guns were shaking in the hands of the soldiers, mostly not fully literate peasant boys, commandeered to the scene and overwhelmed by the tense situation.

If a group of people is surrounded by gun-toting troops, a very natural and quite predictable phenomenon is set in motion, everyone is elbowing his way to the center, for if they start shooting, the ones at the periphery are going to be the first to fall. While we were rearranging our positions, fighting our way to the safety of the middle, the army brought in a convoy of trucks and we were unceremoniously ordered to climb in them. We refused, so a *Securitate* captain pulled out his gun and fired a warning shot. Like lambs, we all got in the trucks. The convoy started rolling to the main road out of town, but three trucks, including the one I was in, were diverted and we headed for the main army barracks in the center of the city. In the yard we were ordered to get off and line up against the wall. Then a line of tanks rolled up in front of us, an armored firing squad. The gunners in the turrets directed their guns at us waiting for the signal to mow us down and thereby set a horrifying example. A lieutenant major was shouting orders at the gunners each time a sergeant delivered new written instructions to him. With each new order the gunners turned and pointed their guns in a different direction, now directly at us, now in some other direction.

I was not afraid, not afraid at all. To the recent flow of testosterone a healthy dose of adrenaline was added and I, like all my colleagues, found myself in agitated, if somewhat confined, motion, shouting slogans "Free the students!", "Free Romania!", "Out with the Russians!". After a short while our fugue of slogans gathered into a concerted chant, we were going to be mowed down in style. We were reenacting an archetypal scene, which we had all so often seen on stage and screen. Just as our chant had developed its very own rhythm and tempo, the tanks started rolling away and we were ordered to climb in the trucks again. So they were not going to stage a massacre in the center of the city, they must have realized that doing so would really trigger an uprising like in Hungary. They are going to drive us out of town and by the roadside, Nazi style, put bullets in our heads. The army lieutenant who was guarding us now on the truck, understood our fright and assured us that we will not be shot, just interned in the army's training barracks at Becicherecul Mic, a dusty little hamlet next to Timişoara. He assured us that the other trucks had also delivered their captives there. This calmed things down a little, though in all truth, I didn't believe this officer, what was he going to tell us, "we have orders to shoot you by the roadside"? We'd have overpowered him and jumped off the truck. The moment we started rolling to our new destination, a very pretty Romanian girl, with smooth silky hair that I remembered rapturously kissing while making love to her a year earlier, asked the question that brought me back to reason "Where are the Kikes now?" I and six others of the fifty or so students on this truck raised our hands and that shut Silky Hairs up. I silently asked myself the corollary to her question, What am I doing here? What business does a Jew have bringing freedom to Romania? Finally, is it at all possible to bring freedom to Romania, even if the Russians would allow that? I started seeing the common answer to my battery of questions — stay away from political causes, no matter how just — just as we arrived in Becicherec as the lieutenant had assured us we would.

The Becicherec army barracks complex consisted of a series of equally spaced parallel long plywood shacks with small paned windows on the sides. Between each pair of neighboring shacks there was a muddy alley just as wide as either of the shacks it separated. Obviously the Romanian army corps of engineers was highly sophisticated in matters of Euclidean geometry, they clearly knew how to draw equally spaced parallel lines and were aware of the fact that such lines don't meet until they reach infinity, which by definition was in enemy territory. The two ends of each alley were guarded by machine guns. Our truck stopped at one end of such an alley and as we got off, we were directed, boys to the shack on our right, girls to the shack on our left. We were warned that the soldiers operating the machine guns had orders to shoot if we as much as open a window, let alone were we to appear at the door. Inside we were provided with large potato sacks and a huge pile of hay which when stuffed into the sacks transformed them into standard issue Warsaw Pact mattresses. It was clear that if Gen. Eisenhower had not yet come to the assistance of the Hungarians, it must have been on account of American intelligence reports about the efficiency of these mattresses in providing Warsaw Pact forces with the kind of restful sleep that rendered them practically invincible. Being confined to these dusty quarters was not quite what we had in mind when marching on Party headquarters, but it was clearly only a temporary setback. It could even be viewed as a victory of sorts, after all they didn't dare shoot us. Obviously the communist authorities were saving us as a bargaining chip for when they finally had to surrender, as we knew they would have to.

In the first hours of our confinement we exchanged messages with the girls in the shack parallel to ours. We spelled them out with our fingers on the windowpanes. The girls were just as agitated and very responsive, but with the two machine guns separating us, these Sabine women weren't available to us either. We made ourselves "beds", they brought us some food and before you knew it dusk had set in. We all lay down on our Warsaw Pact mattresses and an almost perfect quiet descended on our shack, we were all digesting the day's events and trying hard to see the future, our common future, our individual futures. This silence in this ever deeper darkness was hard to bear and people started breaking it. Under the protective cover of darkness one of us finally mustered the courage to speak up "By tomorrow we'll be out of here, they can't keep us here for ever. Their time is up and they know it. When the Americans arrive in Hungary they'll let us go and we'll return like heroes". Then another one went on, and another. We talked like this for hours on end, people started telling their stories, voicing their grievances. Then finally one of us said what was on all our minds, we have to stick together at all costs. We all agreed, and then the oceanic feeling returned. By the time I fell asleep, it was obvious to one and all, in the morning we'll wake up to the noise of the crowd coming to rescue us and to escort us directly to the studios of famous sculptors to pose for a monument memorializing this historic event.

Next morning as I awoke there had been a great change, it was daylight and now when everyone could see you, no one dared speak any longer. The liberating crowds were nowhere to be seen either. I got up and the first thing I noticed was the sizable castor oil stain on my mattress; so much for the invincibility of the Warsaw Pact forces. Suddenly there was a great commotion in the room, a delegation of three army colonels, medical officers and their orderlies showed up. They wanted to know if any of us had tuberculosis or syphilis, so they could isolate them and then they requested that we all give our names and addresses, so they can get us warm clothes for the winter because "we want to get you out of here by next spring". We all signed up and when the doctors left, our mood turned considerably darker. Those three words "by next spring" had the expected chilling effect. Barely an hour later, just time enough to let a good dose of fear invade us, a *Securitate* major showed up and started barking all kinds of wild accusations at us "We know you were planning a counterrevolution, that you wanted to bring down our people's socialist government and that you were carrying weapons. Until we get a complete list of those of you who carried the guns and did the shooting *no one* will leave here". At this he energetically turned around and headed for the door and as he was leaving, turned his head, took a most hateful look at us and repeated the words *"no one, got that? No one!"*

We were all stunned, no one dared say a word, forgotten was last night's "we have to stick together at all costs", gone was the oceanic feeling, not even a pond was left of the "deep and dark blue ocean". For a good hour after these visits we all were on our own. I started assessing my situation. We all knew that none of us had any weapons, and that we didn't shoot. The only shots were fired by the *Securitate* captain, certainly not from a gun provided by us. Obviously they were looking for scapegoats for that communist specialty, the show trial. What were *my* chances for becoming the designated scapegoat? I started devising criteria for picking scapegoats and all these criteria had in common was that I qualified *par excellence* according to each and every criterion. Son of a former capitalist wanting to restore the old regime, a Jew in service of international Zionism, wearer of a goatee proving cosmopolitan reactionary tendencies, and so on, and so on. I could see myself heavily sedated, flanked by two armed *Securitate* officers, before a troyka of illiterate judges, nodding to each of the charges read by the malevolent clerk, eagerly awaiting the judges' choice of the way the death sentence would be carried out, by shooting, by hanging, by stoning, or by some state of the art device. Absorbed in these thoughts, I raised my head and suddenly took notice of the painful frown on Robby's forehead. I nudged him and he looked at me with all the foreboding a nineteen year old can summon. We started whispering and before long were joined by Gyuri Gross, the pharmacist's son. If they seeded scapegoats the way they seed tennis players, Robby, Gyuri and I all qualified as top seed. We were aware of this, all three of us. Coming, as we did, from a culture in which opera played a central role, we proceeded directly to the oath scene. We swore that those of us who make it out of captivity, would devote the rest of their lives to freeing those that were chosen as scapegoats. The rest of the day we just milled around and caught up on the latest rumors. Eisenhower, Eisenhower, what was taking you so long?

On the third day of our captivity the interrogations began. Robby and I prepared an airtight story. We had been at Robby's place studying, when we realized we needed a certain Russian book and then headed for the library. We could have taken the tram, but had forgotten our permits at Robby's place, so we went on foot. Actually we had the worn grey cardboard permits on us, so we tore them up into small pieces and swallowed them. When we got to the bridge, which we had to cross to get to the library, a large crowd, some demonstration in which we had no intention of participating, was also crossing and we were carried away by the current of demonstrators. We rehearsed this story over and over until we knew it by heart. We had answers to all conceivable questions: we needed this particular book, because it contained tables of certain special functions which had appeared in our calculation, because of the cylindrical symmetry of our problem. Once we had these functions, we could proceed to calculate the ....

Our turn came in the early afternoon, virtually simultaneously. I started telling our story, but the bored interrogator couldn't care less. He accepted everything I said and asked but one question, what slogans did the demonstrators shout? "I had to watch not to be trampled by the crowd, so I did not pay much attention, but I think I heard them shout 'out with the Russians'" I replied and the man told me I could go. I went back to my potato sack and soon Robby came as well. His interrogation, same story, another bored guy, who didn't even ask a single question. If they bothered to check out our two stories, there wasn't the slightest inconsistency. Hurrah! So we were not the chosen scapegoats. Everybody else was also all smiles I went to my friend Ionel Petrescu and asked him about his interrogation "my friend so-and-so and I concocted this story that we were accidentally on the bridge and were carried away by the current of demonstrators" he told me. Slowly it emerged that of the two thousand arrested students, nineteen hundred ninety eight were accidentally on the bridge being carried away by the current of two demonstrators. Yet they bought this story. Something was going on and we'll soon know what it was. Maybe the revolution had started for real and the *Securitate* was switching sides so they won't get lynched like in Hungary.

At dusk a *Securitate* colonel announced that we were about to be released. He made a point of explaining to us that in the wake of the rout of "the Hungarian counterrevolutionary thugs", the *Securitate* was releasing us in the dark of night to protect us from the "just fury of the working class". He then announced that there was still a minor formality to be taken care of. We all had to sign the statement "I the undersigned ... hereby state that I have never been arrested by the *Securitate*. I strongly support the government of the Romanian People's Republic and am proud that our people stand united behind it. We shall not condone any counterrevolutionary manifestations." *We* knew we had been arrested, *they* knew we had been arrested, no doubt they would hold it against us in the future, so why this charade? God only knew, but then we all signed it, for who cares why, when freedom beckons.

As it turned out, Khrushchev cared. The Romanian rulers had repeatedly asked the Russian dictator to remove his troops from their country. Now they finally had a beautiful argument, the Hungarians had risen up and Russian boys had to die to crush their uprising. By contrast Romania had proved its total loyalty to the Soviet Union, so this was the ideal time to move the Soviet troops stationed in Romania to neighboring Hungary. Our demonstration was the fly in the ointment. News of it had spread from Timişoara to Bucharest, from there to Western embassies and before you knew it, Voice of America and Radio Free Europe were announcing that the Hungarian uprising had spread to neighboring Romania. The indignant Romanian government denied in the strongest terms this "imperialist calumny" and as proof produced our signed statements. The "imperialist calumniators" found this laughable, but Khrushchev, supposedly a smart cookie, took it at face value and moved his troops to Hungary. Then you wonder why people were later surprised when he thought he'd get away with placing missiles in Cuba, or when he believed he'd make Siberia bloom with Lysenko's mumbo-jumbo. Some months later as the Soviet troops were leaving, all students were marshaled to the railway station to wave the departing troops farewell. For once we relished the task. Whether he knew it or not, from the Romanian vantage point Khrushchev was the good guy. He got the hell out. Understandably the Hungarians saw things somewhat differently. Even as they disagree on who the good guy was, Romanians and Hungarians can agree on the villain of the story. That role clearly fell to General Eisenhower who, to get elected, had spiked his campaign rhetoric with reckless promises he had no intention whatsoever of keeping. These promises cost many people their lives. In my case, thank God, they did not fire. Bless you Fyodor Mikhaikovich.

EXOTIC SPHERES

Mordecai and Sarah Affenschwanz had been communists in Romania before the war, when it was still illegal. Every now and then they considered moving to the Soviet Union just over the border, but Mordecai knew his facts when it came to matters of life and death, and being a Jew in Russia was risky business, case in point his — perish the thought — erstwhile hero Leon Trotsky. Thus stuck in Romania, the Affenschwanzes unquestioningly performed the duties assigned to them by the Party, and managed to survive the war and wave their little red flags at the arriving Russian troops. With communists now in charge, the comrade electrician became involved in matters of government. Much as the future looked bright to him, there was still that name that didn't end in "escu" and Affenschwanz decided he'd rather be a fighter in retirement than a Trotsky in Romania. So in 1950 he and Sarah, retired "for reasons of health" with a fat pension and all the perks of a long-time Party member in good standing. The couple now devoted full time to the career of Tatiana, their only child, an up and coming mathematician. She had regularly won the mathematical Olympics in high school and it was clear she was destined for the sciences. What's more, the privileges of a party-brat did not spoil Tatiana; she still preferred Sarah's gefilte fish to the caviar and foie gras at the Party store.

Following her undergraduate studies in Bucharest, Tatiana was sent on to Moscow. It took some doing, to be sure, but then Sarah, always the Jewish mama, pestered the old communist until he went to the Party

Committee and got his daughter the kind of fellowship she "deserved." There was but one small detail to be settled. In Moscow, there were two great mathematicians working in topology, Tatiana's field of interest. One was a Jew by the name of Moisey Aronovich Eizendrat and the other a true Russian by the name of Lev Ivanovich Vatagin. Mordecai counseled Tatiana to opt for the goy. "You never know what can happen to a Jew. Stay away from him, you go for the ...gin whatever his name. He is good. Right? So what else do you want?" He had a point. After all, Vatagin was an academician with all the many privileges that entailed, while Eizendrat, famous as he may have been at Harvard and in Paris, was still only a corresponding member of the Academy, a much less exalted position. "And then," Mordecai added, "just don't get into any more trouble. You don't always have to say what you think. Here, we could help, like the time you had to prove to that professor of yours that his theorem was 'predicated on a fallacy' in a public seminar of all places ... Luckily the bastard did not have connections. But there, in Moscow, you're on your own, completely on your own."

So Tatiana registered at Moscow University and with her credentials, "Gin," the academician, accepted her. Let it be emphasized that this was no mean feat, given Gin's dislike of Jews, but then old Gin came from a family of officers, his father had been a colonel in the imperial army and would have made it to general like his father and grandfather before him, had it not been for the revolution during which he gave his "life for the Tsar." With such a background, Gin stuck to topology and never quibbled about students sent to him by the Party. "Always ready, like the little red-scarfed pioneers, I am", he used to say concerning service to the Party, while at the same time gesturing surrender. So it is that in the summer of 1956 we find Tatiana Affenschwanz studying "exotic spheres," in Moscow of all places. Gin tried to talk her into something more mundane, but Tatiana was enraptured with her exotic spheres. "You can reshape them into ordinary spheres but never smoothly," is the way she put it.

"Watch out this is very abstract stuff, discovered in America . . . reactionary?" Gin would inveigh, but in vain. Tatiana was committed. Her father didn't die for the Tsar, she could afford commitment. Hadn't Mordecai and Sarah been committed to, well Trotsky, yes, but also to Stalin and done quite well by their commitments? Retirement "for reasons of health," true, but with access to the Party store, not too bad after all. So

Tatiana stuck to her exotic spheres and decided to size them up, to see what distance you could travel on such spheres and where such travel might lead. She was quite successful and by October had found what looked like the right concept for this exotic distance.

Other than topology her everyday life was rather routine. She was staying at a special dormitory for well-connected students, with elaborate security arrangements: round the clock security police to ward off undesirable outsiders and to trap the restless insiders. On every floor there was a *matyushka*, a floor-mother who saw after the students' well-being. She dispensed that ultimate Soviet consumer item: toilet paper. To be sure, you had to have a serious case of diarrhea, preferably accompanied by verifiable vomiting, before Pelageia, Tatiana's *matyushka*, would hand you a roll of the valuable stuff, but then you could luxuriate, and forget the rigid hardness of Pravda and Izvestia, the poor man's toilet accessories. Rumor had it that Pelageia peddled most of the tissue on the black market, but that the authorities were willing to close an eye in view of her valuable supervisory services.

In the evening Tatiana, when done with her exotica, would participate in one of the conversations in the big hall of the dormitory. A Hungarian biologist, one János Vékony a gentle lad, blond, tall, of good stock (his father an assistant minister of commerce, a former Nazi Arrowhead now reformed into a not necessarily Jew-hating member of the Hungarian Communist elite) had developed a crush on Tatiana. Well, even if János' attitude towards Jews was one of doctrinaire impartiality, he could not resist Tatiana. And you couldn't blame him, for her tall, somewhat clumsy, yet charming frame housed a pair of dark eyes aglow with the kind of intensity that continuous concentration on exotic spheres exacts from the Jewish soul. Add to this her sensuous lips and you will see some merit to the *matyushka* system, whereby János and Tatiana conversed in the hall, monitored by a "social host's" watchful eyes and open ears. This way the two youngsters could concentrate on the things that matter: exotic spheres and Lysenko-biology. Remove the *matyushka* and remove the social host and what have you got? Exotic spheres? Maybe, but certainly not the kind young socialist mathematicians should be studying, if already they have to study them against advice from highest authority.

It was at one of these evening conversations that Tatiana's sudden downfall was set in motion. That afternoon Gin had finally accepted her ideas on distance relations on exotic spheres and asked her for a properly written version to submit to the *Doklady*, the journal of the Academy, no less. Defended orally, the paper would earn Tatiana her title of Candidate in the Mathematical Sciences, with a coveted Doctorate to follow. Gin had prided himself of never having had a Jew earn a title at his institute. "Let them go to Eizendrat and learn Jewish maths, here we do the Russian thing," he would say. Now for Tatiana he had prepared a defense: "Well, she's a lady," at which his eyes would roguishly twinkle, "a lady first" while his statement would conclude "and she is a well-connected lady ... highest recommendations, if you know what I mean."

Anyway, Tatiana was on the march and nothing short of a catastrophe could stop her. But that catastrophe was in the making. That evening she radiantly told János in the hall, "Soon you'll be addressing me as comrade candidate." The well-connected biologist, in spite of his infatuation, turned deaf to Tatiana's happy tidings. He was the embodiment of gloom and doom. "Come on, didn't you hear what I said?" the girl went on. "Anyway, what's wrong with you?" The blond lad looked indignantly at Tatiana and like in a dream mumbled the words, "My brother is dead."

Barely had he uttered these words when the "social host" came over to offer his sympathy in the form of a glass of kvas and then considerately joined the couple. Tatiana would have been well advised to heed this ominous signal, but shocked out of her jubilant mood, as she was, she did what she did best: concentrate on the matter at hand. It was clear to her, as it must have been to the "social host" as well, that the young Hungarian's presumably young brother hadn't just suddenly dropped dead of ill health. After all, János had never expressed the slightest worry on this count. So with the events in Hungary — this was October 1956, after all— there was hardly any doubt that the fellow must have met a violent death. Tatiana, ever so precise in her mathematical terminology, asked the first deviationist question, "Was your brother a freedom fighter?"

"You mean a counterrevolutionary," the social host reprovingly interjected, as if to emphasize "we'll keep the discussion clean in my hall." János looked on disoriented while Tatiana admitted the correction with a "well whatever, . . . was he?"

At this point the "social host" expressed his insistence with a severe look in Tatiana's direction, but kept his silence because he also wanted to hear the answer. It suddenly became obvious to him that this evening was out of the ordinary and that he would have to file a report. As long as he would have to go to all that trouble, and have his own loyalty extensively examined in the process, he might as well have some juicy material to report.

Under the stress of silence, János now explained, "My brother, he is, ... I mean he was seven years older than I. He worked for the Interior Ministry." In other words, he had been a police agent.

Both Tatiana and the "social host" knew that in Hungary angry people were lynching all the police agents they could lay their hands on, and János' brother obviously hadn't hidden out well enough. A slight though audible sigh of relief was the "social host's" sign of approval. János' brother had been a "good guy" after all and mourning was ideologically justifiable under the circumstances. He was about to leave the young couple to its sadness when Tatiana blurted out in visible anger the unexpected, the unacceptable, the ideologically dangerous. "Your brother was working for the police ... How come you never mentioned this before? .... Well, he for the police, you for Lysenko ... a nice family, I must admit. Were he not your brother ..." — at this point her voice grew shaky with emotion — "I would have to say, serves him right ...." Had she but stopped here, she could still have weaseled out of it by pretending all she meant was "serves him right for his lack of vigilance" or "serves him right for his careless neglect of security" or something along these lines. But no, Tatiana had to go all the way and complete her sentence with the two words that were to seal her fate "....the scoundrel."

Where did these words come from? Tatiana read the newspapers and like everybody else she tried to divine the truth between the subtle lies in Pravda and Scinteia, both freely available at the dorm. But she never spent much time on politics. Her concentration was claimed by less Byzantine matters like exotic spheres. Yet somehow she filtered the information gleaned from the press through her methodological and strictly logical mind, and unconsciously, there is no doubt about that, the results affected her emotions. Reason can be the main enemy of the individual. It interferes with the natural flow of the reflexes. It can even create its own reflexes that can unexpectedly emerge at the most embarrassing moments and reveal that which is best kept secret, hidden from external scrutiny. It is an imperfection of our species that the functions of reason and emotion, which so completely shape our lives, are housed in the same organ and thus can interfere with each other. But this is the result of a lengthy evolutionary process and it must be good for something. Whatever that may be, it certainly was not studying mathematics in Moscow in the Fifties.

Once the fatal words had been uttered, a deep silence settled in the hall. The "social host" knew he would have to destroy Tatiana, he knew he had the power to do so, but unlike the conceited usher who keeps the person with the wrong ticket away from the show, he was not gloating. This was much more serious. There was no way Tatiana could now purchase the right ticket for a future show, for any show. He had seen it all before: human beings from far-away lands self-destructing in front of him because faulty wiring somewhere in their brains allowed that explosive mixture of reason and emotion to form and to blow up what looked like a most promising career, a most happy life. As if to stress the finality of that which had just transpired, the "social host" excused himself and returned to his "business," attending to the kvas. János, also aware of all this and of the extra pain the loss of Tatiana would cause in his life, could only come up with an angry "You fool." At that he gulped down his kvas and left, obviously more concerned with survival than with the object of his love-interest.

Tatiana spent the night in a state of what may rightly be described as creative agitation. She realized she was in trouble, deep trouble, and yet this did not in any way inhibit her, paralyze her. Her reason and emotions, dwelling as they do in the same organ, interfered, but constructively, for a change (evolution?). Her emotions, strained to the extreme, made way for reason to take over, and in the course of one tense night, interrupted only by three doses of very black coffee that Tatiana, as in a dream, consumed from her worn turquoise plastic cup, she set up the whole framework of lemmas and theorems that fleshed out those ideas, which in a more intuitive vein she had successfully defended before Gin. Even a significant new corollary of her main theorem was derived and it was all set down in a paper. Written in her cryptic style it was a masterpiece of economic reasoning, yet sufficiently well started to involve the educated reader from the very first line, as in a detective story. All that remained to be done was to fill in the references to the literature and she could do that the next morning in the library in an hour or two. As the morning sun bathed her gray room in golden hues, she lay down for an hour or so, unable to sleep, in the knowledge that a beautiful piece of work had been completed, thoughts of János ' brother still comfortably repressed. Around nine, she left the dorm.

The doorman's booth was unattended. After a stop at the library, with the references all properly filled in, she went to Gin's office. He was temporarily detained at a faculty meeting but before lunch saw Tatiana and took her paper for a critical reading.

It was shortly thereafter, at 12:45 to be precise, that Tatiana was called to the Party office. The moment she saw the dean of students it became clear even to this active mathematician that something of great impact was about to happen. Accompanied by the old dean in his worn gray suit, the young lady proceeded to the third floor where the secretary of the Party Committee, one Sergey Vassilievich Bezchastny, a sweaty yellow-skinned man with a few strands of colorless hair drawing a fine abstract picture on his shiny baldness, received her by lowering his eyes onto a somewhat greasy piece of paper to which a copy of Tatiana's passport picture was attached with a paper clip.

"Comrade Affenschwanz," Secretary Bezchastny solemnly intoned, "it has come to our attention that you hold reactionary views on the counter-revolution in the Hungarian People's Republic. Such views are damaging to the interests of the USSR, the host country that so generously offers you the benefit of its scientific facilities. Your lack of gratitude aside, such views are dangerous and inadmissible in a socialist society. We have therefore decided to give you seven days in which to settle your affairs here and return to your homeland." At this the Party secretary established eye contact with the lady expert in exotic spheres, and in so doing raised his head as if to deny her the benefit of the light reflected into her eyes by his polished scalp.

Tatiana protested. "I have my thesis ready. Could I at least have my oral exam?"

"Seven days comrade, seven days. Good bye" came the final reply. Presently the dean of students got up and Tatiana knew the decision was irrevocable.

The devastated woman now saw her one hope in her sponsor. Yet Gin was a changed man the next time she encountered him. The descendant of generals knew how to kick a begging leper without establishing physical contact with the diseased person.

"Comrade Affenschwanz, I have read the cute paper you left with me. It develops the abstract idea of an American mathematician. In my most reasoned view" — he repeated these words as if to simultaneously wash his hands of Tatiana's fate and of the hold her exciting personality had exercised over him only the day before — "in my most reasoned view this paper is not up to the standards of Soviet mathematics and as such it unfortunately does not qualify for publication in *Doklady.*"

"How about my candidate's exam?"

"No" came the curt answer from the grand old man now totally immersed in his work. Tatiana took her paper from Gin's desk and slowly walked out of the office as if hit by a bolt of lightning. She wandered aimlessly down the familiar bright corridor with the red stone floor and the whitewashed walls, turned the corner, and suddenly found herself in the "Eizendrat Wing." At this point an idea crossed her mind. "How about talking to the Jew?" Her father's words, "You go to that '. . . gin' whatever his name" echoed in her mind as she stopped in front of the Jew's office. With the single-mindedness that follows a sleepless night she knocked at Moisey Aronovich's door and as luck would have it, the small, stocky topologist was at his desk, deep in thought.

"Professor Eizendrat," she didn't dare address him Academician Eizendrat, he wasn't, he was but a corresponding member and unlike most of his peers he did not pretend, or have to pretend. Wherever there was true mathematics, people knew the name M.A. Eizendrat unadorned by any official title. "Professor Eizendrat," Tatiana repeated a minute or so later. The third try proved more successful. The professor looked up, shifted his horn-rimmed glasses, smiled, and with a conspiratorial expression exclaimed "Exotic spheres, . . . very exotic spheres, . . . so I have heard."

"What do I do now?" Tatiana asked in desperation.

"First things first. Let's hear your results." Tatiana couldn't believe her ears. She was being sent in exile and the corresponding member wanted to talk exotic business. But the adrenaline was flowing and with her impulsive elegance Tatiana treated Eizendrat to a lively forty-minute lecture on her work. More precisely, she lectured for the first few minutes and then Eizendrat kept asking "right question" after "right question" and they built up the whole edifice essentially from his inquiries. When it all stood, the little man exclaimed, "This is a beautiful piece of work." It was an honest expression of pleasure, of admiration, so unlike Gin's "cute."

"So what are you going to do with it?" Eizendrat asked and then answered his own question. "I guess you're going to publish it as fast as you can, before somebody scoops you. How about *Doklady?*"

"Professor Vatagin . . ." in front of Eizendrat Tatiana spitefully demoted the full Academician, which elicited another smile from the Jewish topologist " … Professor Vatagin has told me he didn't find it worthy of any Soviet journal."

"My dear Tatiana Mordechaievna, Academician Vatagin is a well-known … son of a bitch. What he meant to say was that *Doklady* and other Russian journals are closed to you. So, publish the paper elsewhere."

"Like where?"

"Like …. in the *Journal of Modern Algebra*."

"But my paper is not on Modern Algebra, or any algebra for that matter."

"I know, I know, …. but you see my dear I publish there too, as do Professors Gol'denberg, and Glyukshtern, and none of us works in algebra. You see JMA is not a Russian journal, in the sense of Academician Vatagin. Yet this is one of the most famous journals abroad … Academician Vatagin had once wanted to close it for 'scientific reasons.' He argued the same way as you just did, and concluded that papers on topology, number theory, symbolic logic, etc. etc…. do not belong in a journal supposedly devoted to algebra. But the publishing house kept the journal because it earns more hard currency than ten Russian journals put together."

"I would be very grateful if you accepted my paper for JMA."

"Consider it done. Anything else?"

"How about a candidate degree?" Tatiana gambled.

"I expected that. They sent you home and Academician Vatagin I presume canceled your exam, isn't that it?" Tatiana nodded. "Alas, here I can be of no help. If I took you on as a student, right away I would be accused of stealing Academician Vatagin's best … or should I say most controversial ….student. In my time I weathered worse accusations. If your name is well known in Paris and at Garvard University, believe me Tatiana Mordechaievna, they think twice before they send you to Siberia or wherever. But say we did the paperwork tomorrow and scheduled your exam for the day after, I wouldn't be surprised if you would be expelled as of to-morrow rather than a week hence. Had you been my student …. I would have seen to it that you had proper instruction in how not to shoot off that clever mouth of yours . . . but the harm has been done and it is now incumbent on us to salvage whatever can be salvaged. So the paper gets published and you go back to Bulgaria …."

119

"Romania, Professor Eizendrat."

"...Romania ... and you promise, a solemn promise, that you will keep your head high and continue doing what anybody with your brain is meant to do."

This optimistic advice was easier given than followed. For much as all of "Garvard" University may have been talking about Tatiana Affenschwanz's guide to the exotic spheres, that celebrated young author once back in her homeland was now the bleeding dolphin in a pool of sharks.

Her troubles reflected upon the whole Affenschwanz clan. Mordecai's health was suddenly found improved by the retirement commission and he was summoned back to work as an electrician at a hospital for the mentally ill. Of course this entailed the loss of the pension and of the access to the Party store, as well as a move from the comfortable apartment on the Boulevard to two rooms in a slum, a *mahala*. Worst of all, these two rooms were in a five-room apartment which had to be shared with a family of three including a new born baby, and with a whore who used her room as her place of business. The only advantage to this apartment was that on account of the thin walls the Affenschwanzes could not go about the loud business of apportioning blame without being overheard, which was hardly desirable. Thus they could quarrel to their hearts' content only on those rare occasions, when during a walk through the more isolated spots of the Cismigiu, Bucharest's Central Park, they could be sure of being out of hearing range of just about everybody.

Tatiana herself could find no meaningful employment, not even as a high school teacher. Her qualifications were always eagerly applauded, but the moment the personnel office received her file, the job would suddenly disappear. She was not denied access to the University's mathematics library and used her time well. She completed another paper on exotic spheres but much to her chagrin the manuscript she sent to Eizendrat got lost in the mail. Eizendrat sent her a supportive letter but it was clear he was doing it out of decency rather than in answer to any communication from Tatiana. On the first anniversary of her homecoming, Tatiana's unemployment marked her as a social parasite and, her parents' valiant efforts notwithstanding, she was deported to a forced labor camp.

The day after the deportation of his daughter, Mordecai went to a very high Party official, a "comrade" from the old days, a Romanian, and begged him to do something for the ill-fated girl. "Look Affenschwanz, Jews ...

you know I am not anti-Semitic, not that I love Jews but anyway, ... Jews, always have some money, real money, not our *lei*," the official started. Then he went on, "You must have a relative somewhere — Israel, the U.S.A., ... Honduras, ... what do I know, some second cousin of your late father's aunt ...."

"No, we have absolutely no family in the West, absolutely none."

"Still, should a long-forgotten relative suddenly turn up or should you otherwise be able to arrange for five hundred dollars to be deposited each month to a certain account at a certain bank in Bern, then I can guarantee to you that Tatiana will leave for the country of her choice. Then, two months after the first deposit is made you will be reinstated in the Party with pension, Party store privileges, everything. How does this seem to you? ... Fair I should say, right?"

"There's but one rub, we have nobody to make the deposit."

"There's always a way. Why don't you talk it over with Sarah, how is the old girl anyway?"

"Thanks, fine."

"Well, talk it over with her and I'll see what can be done."

Mordecai returned dejected, desperate. It took the Affenschwanzes three more months and a letter from Moscow University Professor Eizendrat before they even obtained a permit to visit their only child, their high hope, in the carrot farm somewhere in the Bărăgan where she was atoning for her parasitism. The visit, a painful one, was as it turned out, the last opportunity the adoring parents got to see the expert in exotic spheres. They took a long walk along the farm's fence and softly conversed, using as many Yiddish words as possible. Even had the guards overheard them as they should have, they would hardly have understood what was being said. Shedding the kind of tears next of kin are likely to succumb to at funerals, the heavy-hearted parents left the camp.

At this point Tatiana's trace becomes murky; it dissolves as it were into thin air. To believe the official version recorded in the Bucharest newspapers, a routine inspection tour of the Bărăgan farms by the director of the carrot section at the Ministry of Agriculture ended in tragedy in the spring of 1958. Discovering irregularities indicative of sabotage at one farm, the vigilant director tracked them down to their source, an "exotic lady parasite with counterrevolutionary leanings." Given the lax security arrangements at the farm, the "exotic lady" pulled a gun, and in the ensuing scuffle, the saboteur seriously wounded the official, but a second bullet she fired ricocheted from a tree into her own back, and, as if endowed with a sense of justice of its own, lodged itself in her treacherous heart. The stories named neither the vigilant director of the carrot section nor the "exotic lady" as she came to be known, nor were the news accounts accompanied by photographs of the victim or of the villainess. The only other detail provided was that the still nameless parents of the "exotic lady" vehemently condemned her treason and thus earned themselves full rehabilitation (effective September 12, 1958).

The rumors floating in Bucharest gave a more detailed and rather differently flavored rendition of a similar incident. Tatiana was explicitly named, though the carrot director was still left anonymous. Apparently he was a married man with anywhere from two to five children. Yet this, on the face of it, good husband and father, had made it a custom to top his inspection trips with certain, well, let's call them parties, to which he would bring a dozen or so of his closest collaborators and friends, and to which the farm was to provide the female touch. The local peasant girls would as a rule gratefully accept such an invitation, well aware of the implied honor. Apparently at the last such "party" a Jewish "exotic lady" had been summoned simply on account of her good looks, and when she put up resistance, one of the guards of this "parasite farm," himself a "party guest," pulled a gun and unloaded five shots into the lady's heart. According to this version the carrot director could not be named, for he had never been wounded and the authorities bought the silence of the late "exotic lady's" parents by restoring them to political favor.

It is hard to make much sense out of either of these two accounts, even as they agree on the "exotic lady's" tragic fate. On the other hand much in life is irrelevant and what counts in the end are ideas or beauty which survive and can be bequeathed to posterity. So it may be of interest to know what happened to the geometry of exotic spheres after the demise of its leading practitioner. Like most viable ideas, it found a new champion, also a woman, appointed to a chair at the University of Bern on the basis of one published paper and of a superlative letter of recommendation from the distinguished Russian mathematician M.A. Eizendrat. This young lady-professor lived the life of an almost total recluse, except for her teaching activities and her attendance of certain seminars and symposia. Thus very little was known about her even in provincial Bern. The only other piece of information available on this peculiar character was, that in the morning of the twelfth day of every month (or a day or two earlier if the twelfth happened to fall on a weekend or holiday) she would pay a visit to the local branch of a well-known bank.

THE TREASURE HUNTERS' BURDENS

Titus never says anything new. His typical story is always about someone I can't even remember any longer, say A, who was with us in elementary school, then went on to marry B, the daughter of C, who had an apartment three blocks away from where we are standing right now, from which C moved away twenty years ago, and which was then occupied by the D's, who.... You get the rest. Nothing ever happens in Titus' stories, they just drift in a cloud of irrelevance in between the dramatic stops he makes in his walk, extending both his arms as if to catch some meaning sprinkled from up high by the god of storytellers.

I am not trying to be hard on Titus, after all without him this whole story would never have come into being, but if it did, it did so by happenstance, not by design.

I had not come to the shores of the Bega, just because that's where I was born. I had come to meet my friend Traian Mărgineanu. Yes, around here, unlike me, most males start life with the first name of one Roman emperor or another, no Neros or Caligulas though, and stuttering Claudius is in short supply as well. Traian assured me he could find the object I was after. It was a sizeable piece of parchment on which my great-great great-grandfather had written in his exquisite calligraphy the tale of his move to Temesvar from his native Bukovina. He had left his shtetl near Chernowitz on the rumor, that in the Habsburg Empire Temesvar was the ideal place for a Jew. It was not only touted as civilized, but the word pogrom, so it was said, was unknown thereabouts. The only danger was in the getting there. Pulling a cart with his wares this remote ancestor of mine was attacked by the betyars, who took with them his whole cart, leaving him destitute from one moment to the next. But then His Apostolic Majesty's Hussars rode their Arabian horses in pursuit of the thieves, recovered the whole loot, and returned it to its rightful owner. That's civilization for you on the road to a place where the word pogrom was yet to have been introduced by the fellow with the square mustache.

It is at this point on the parchment that a map is drawn by the same careful hand indicating the point at which this grateful travelling salesman buried his parents' wedding rings and a two karat diamond solitaire to mark the spot at which his belief in human decency had been restored. Along with the heirlooms he also buried, so the calligraphic text said, "a document of great value to my descendents." He wanted all this retrieved by these descendents, if, in the long run, all else in Temesvar also worked out this well.

I had seen this parchment once in my life, on the very day in the late Fifties when I left this then so unhappy land. My father took the parchment out of the bureau where he had kept it hidden under his shirts all these years. It was his wish to burn it there and then in the Canadian stove whose fire was keeping us warm on this grey November day. "Better burn it than leave it to these bastards," was the way he put it. Busy with more important matters, he gave me the parchment to burn. I simply couldn't bring myself to carry out this barbaric act, and gave the parchment instead to my … what should I call her? Girlfriend would cast an aura of undeserved innocence on her, whereas mistress, though maybe more accurate, would sound ungentlemanly. So let me just call her Mirela with one l as required by the phonetic spelling of the modern Romanian language.

For the thirty years following this transfer of the parchment, I had lost contact with Mirela, and for all I know some grazing Ukrainian or Hungarian cow may have chipped a tooth on a two-karat solitaire.

After '89 with the Ceauşescus murdered in the very way they would have approved of for anyone but themselves, I dared show my face in the city of my youth. Titus was there and so was Traian, Mirela however went missing.

I asked around, and my reward was a flood of words that added up to nothing beyond a fast spoken, indeed fast-shouted complaint, repeated over and over by everyone I met, "My life has been stolen from me."

In the middle of a story about the G family's demise, of the G family residing in the Josefin district, right next to the H's who married off their son to....., Titus, motivated simply by the chain of name-connections that was his specialty, unintentionally dropped Mirela's name. There were no cousins or siblings to continue the chain after Mirela. All she was needed for in the chain was to introduce the County hospital in which she met a horrible end in the mid-seventies, in the very wing under the direction of Dr. L, the one whose wife was involved in a call-girl ring, along with....

With Mirela dead, all hope for recovering the parchment seemed lost. But then, hope springs eternal, as they say for good reason, and I found hope again through Traian,

"Sure, Mirela died at the County hospital, they killed her there. Dr. L had one of his fits — you know he was insane — while operating on Mirela, and he cut her insides to pieces as if they were mincemeat. Heavily sedated, she survived for another twenty-four hours and then breathed her last, may God rest her in peace. But as far as the parchment you are looking for, that's neither here nor there. By then she had long surrendered it to Captain Grigorescu to save her son from detention. She had told me so herself the last time I saw her. Grigorescu then detained her son all the same. They say he was badly tortured."

"Who is this Captain Grigorescu?"

"He was the most vicious of the *Securitate* men in all the Banat. A chain-smoker he loved to extinguish his cigarettes on his victims' arms or faces. He was known for his passionate smile when inhaling the odor of charred human flesh. They say, he used to have orgasms when doing so." I could trust Traian, for of all the friends I left behind in Romania, he is the only one who behaved in a principled manner, he did not join the Communist Party, much as this ruined his chances for a career. By contrast Titus and even Mirela had joined the Party for reasons Titus admits as having been purely opportunistic. It was what everybody did, and you cannot begrudge them. I wander what one of those Party meetings must have been like with not one true communist among the participants, but just a bunch of opportunistic phonies. They tried to pressure Traian to join, but to his credit he stood his ground.

"You knew Grigorescu?" I asked Traian.

"He used to sit next to me at the opera. He was a quite cultured person. He invited me once to their headquarters on Loga Row to listen to a recording of *Il Trovatore* from La Scala. It was real eerie. During the dungeon scene, along with the soprano you could hear moans of intense pain from the corridor. Then the thuds of hard fist-blows would elicit a shrill shout and finally silence. I didn't dare say anything, and concentrated instead on the music, Fedora Barbieri was Azucena."

"Is this Grigorescu still around today? Anyway, what would his interest have been in my parchment?"

"Mirela made a major mistake, she talked about it and about the location of a treasure to which it supposedly held the clue."

"I told her not to!"

"And yes, Grigorescu is still around. After the revolution, he purchased the soap factory on the Titu Maiorescu Quay in the industrial district. It's the biggest soap factory in the country and he is raking in the money. He then branched out into hotels and now owns a whole hotel chain, the *Perinița*."

"How could he have had the money to purchase a factory?"

"Burning holes in human flesh was a lucrative business under the communists. People were prepared to pay up to make the pain stop. Besides, if you knew a little dirt on the asset liquidator's past, the price of the asset you wished to purchase would sink fast, and Grigorescu knew a lot of dirt about lots of people, don't worry."

"Is there a way I could see this Grigorescu and get the parchment back from him?"

"You can meet him at his factory, he is known to spend his mornings there. Your parchment? That's another question, but be warned, I have yet to meet someone who managed to get anything from Grigorescu. He is a taker, not a giver."

"What have I got to lose? I'll give it a try."

The very next morning, unannounced — surprise is the best strategy in such matters — I put in an appearance at Grigorescu's office. It was a spacious room with high ceilings, its tall windows looking out at the muddy waters of the Bega. The walls were covered with bookcases on which documents of dubious origin, certainly not books, were arranged in what looked like alphabetical order. Large yellow markers indicated the spots where a new initial took over.

In their heart of hearts, communist torturers always had a soft spot for the ever joyous Americans. Now that the Cold War was over with the well-known outcome, this soft spot has matured into outright reverence. As such I, by now an American, was received like a Rockefeller. A Turkish coffee and a glass of mineral water were placed in front of me, without my asking or even being asked. While I took a sip of the black liquid, making sure not to stir the sediment, the former *Securitate* captain lit a Marlborough, and started shaking its ashes into a porcelain ashtray in the shape of a human face, its cheeks in a passable approximation of flesh color, worn off here and there from the extinction of too many cigarettes over the years.

"Ah, that parchment, I remember it only too well. What a romantic story! I even made a trip to Transylvania and had the ground dug up where the drawing implied the valuables should be hidden. I came away empty-handed. It was quite an embarrassment, and there were the two men who had done the digging. I learned later that they were known subversives and therefore had to be liquidated. I still reproach myself for not having been able to save their lives." He forcefully put out a cigarette on the ashtray's left cheek.

"So, where is the parchment now?" I asked.

"Who knows where! Anyway, it's of no use to you, so what do you care?" He looked at me in visible irritation, as one looks at someone who brings up a painful topic that one considered settled, closed for good.

"It's an heirloom, a bit of valuable family history."

"Look, Sir, take it from one who lived history, closed chapters should just be left that way, they should under no circumstances be reopened. You never know what monster you may be unleashing." Another cigarette, this one only half smoked was being extinguished. It was clear that the act of extinction was more pleasurable to this man than the act of smoking, no visible or audible orgasms though.

It was at this moment that Traian, as we had agreed before the visit, entered the office to a warm greeting from the captain,

"Mr. Mărgineanu, what a pleasure to see you. Remember when we listened to that marvelous *Rigoletto* at my apartment?"

"It was *Il Trovatore*."

"That's right, so it was. With Fedora Barbieri. I remember now."

"And it was on Loga Row, at your office."

"On Loga Row? I never had an office there." His voice rose in what was unmistakable anger, as he kept repeating, "On Loga Row, of all places. Never! Nevvver!" A cigarette with only one puff inhaled from it was being furiously put out on the ashtray's virgin lips. "Gentlemen, I am sorry, but I must take my leave now. Business calls!" The captain rose and started ushering us to the door. He opened it and we then also rose and let ourselves be ushered out.

On our way back towards the Haymarket, Traian shared with me a crucial observation,

"Did you see all those files on the wall? Those are certainly no soap contracts. Must be his old files, the ones he uses to put pressure on people these days. They are nicely alphabetized and looking at the shelf where your name would be, I saw something that looked a lot like a parchment. Did you notice that?" I hadn't, but then I was mostly watching the face in the ashtray.

Whose could that parchment have been? Good question! How is one to get an answer? What was needed was a private eye, send Mary Astor to Humphrey Bogart. Humphrey Bogart in Timişoara? Let's stop kidding, maybe a Dracula or a Tarzan but no Sam Spade. Yet, along Griselini Street on the way to Dome Square, right next to the Courthouse you encounter the badly worn advertisement for the office of "Sabin Spătaru, private detective." This bald and fat man's expertise lies in catching straying spouses in the act, the kinkier the better. Parchments in soap factories? Let's be serious! But this close to a courthouse, "serious" has a well-defined meaning somewhere beyond two thousand Euros. I was willing to put up the money and at the very least the man showed common sense,

"I know who this Grigorescu is. You can be sure he does not keep any incriminating documents in his soap-factory office. I don't know what a parchment is doing in a soap factory, but I do know that you cannot enter this man's office without getting caught. This is a former *Securitate* big boss, and I am sure he employs his former subordinates as current watchdogs. Fortunately among these, there is one Camil Ciocârlie, whose brother Cezar works for me. I can show some money to Cezar, and he'll either do it himself, or get Camil to do it for him, never mind Grigorescu. The beauty is that among these people, money not only speaks, but it speaks a language that is clearly understood by all."

With such an easy inroad to Grigorescu's shelves, in forty-eight hours I was holding in my hands a copy of the parchment spotted by Traian. It was my parchment in that it was written in my ancestor's beautiful Gothic calligraphy, but it also wasn't, for it lacked the map and the text referring to this map. It looked as if it were of absolutely no use, hardly worth the five-thousand Euros I ended up paying for it. Yet a closer examination of this incomplete copy had two features of its own, missing in the original. These features turned out to be more useful at this point than any map could possibly have been. Embedded in the curlicues of the opening calligraphic Gothic capital H was clearly visible the name Mirela, and this name was rendered in my former mistress' unmistakable childish handwriting, without the slightest trace of Gothic affectations. This was as good an authentication as anyone could possibly have wished. More importantly, once the author gets to his mugging by the betyars, an undoubtedly recent addition appears. Where my ancestor, a fine calligrapher but hardly a talented stylist, mentions the word betyar, for the sixth time in three lines of text, something I remember with a smile from my original reading of the document some five decades ago, a name now makes it onto the parchment, a name ending in "escu" and thereby shouting to high heaven its anachronistic apparition. It is the name Petrescu. Here is Sam Spade's take on this Petrescu,

"That is Leontin Petrescu. Like everyone hereabouts, I know only too well this infamous name. Petrescu was Grigorescu's aide referred to as 'the finisher' in the Ceauşescu days, for it was he who was given the task to finish off those detainees who were neither of any further use, nor fit to be released into society. All Petrescu was called on to do, was to liquidate these detainees, and thereafter get the *Securitate*'s doctor to certify their demise as a 'tragic accident.' It was said that unlike his boss, this Petrescu experienced orgasm not by extinguishing cigarettes in the detainees living bodies, but by copulating with those bodies after he had extinguished all traces of life in them with a shot in the head."

"Can we find him somewhere? Would it be safe to pay him a visit?"

"A man as universally reviled as Petrescu cannot be employed these days, not even by his satisfied former boss. They probably handed him a nice sum and ordered him to keep a low profile. He supposedly made a successful switch from necrophilia to drug addiction, and with the money at his command lives in a Ronaţ slum dwelling on one of the unpaved side-streets of one of the pothole filled asphalted side-streets of Bogdăneştilor. If you want, I can arrange a visit, but it'll cost you some more Euros."

"Is it safe?"

"I'll be there with you and keep in mind, the man is not an assassin, he's but a cowardly murderer, knowing he's being watched."

We went to Ronaţ on a hot and humid afternoon. The cab took us to the pothole-filled asphalted side-street, and from there on we continued on foot along its unpaved feeder. We got to a low one-floor house painted in deep blue, with a corridor facing the street and leading back to the living- and bed-rooms and further back through a kitchen and bathroom into the garden. The man of the house was sitting in the corridor in a deep and well-padded armchair soiled with sweat. Two ottomans flanked this chair and we understood without any explicit invitation that we were meant to sit on them. Petrescu was in what seemed to be a trance, he must have taken drugs, most likely heroin.

Sam Spade started the conversation. "Listen Petrescu, we know you had something to do with Grigorescu's parchment. What did you do with it? Did you go to the place indicated on its map?"

"It's hot today. Let me rest. Don't bother me with that old crap." And he went on watching the street. A bicycle just rode by and had raised a cloud of dust. With loud breaths Petrescu seemed to inhale the dry dust like someone doing coke.

"It may be old crap to you, but it is of paramount interest to my client here. We brought you some cocaine and some heroin but you must earn them." At the mention of his favorite drugs, Petrescu seemed to muster some attention, but it dissipated fast and in no time he was back in his trance.

"Did you go to that spot on the map?"

"Yes I did, so what?"

"What did you find there?"

"Nothing, absolutely nothing" he replied with no affect whatsoever in his voice.

"That does not sound very convincing."

"I don't give a fuck whether you are convinced or not. I found nothing."

I exchanged looks with Sam Spade. Was this no more than an expensive dead end? Then Petrescu moaned deeply and thinking he had lost the offered gift with his negative replies, added,

"The old Jew who wrote that parchment in that weird script of his, had something in mind, but I don't know what. I arrested two old Jews and had them read it over and over, but even they could make no sense out of it. Had to liquidate the both of them, just to make sure they won't be talking about the parchment. One of them insisted it was in code, the whole parchment and even the map. Nonsense, I say, Jewish nonsense, Jewish crap." As he spoke these insulting words, Petrescu looked in my direction and threw his mouth ajar in something that might have resembled a sarcastic smile, had he any frontal teeth left. Short of those teeth — he obviously had the money, though he lacked the will to go to a dentist — it was no more than a pathetic display of cowardly neglect. As the smile was leaving his face and his mouth firmly closing up, Petrescu returned to his trance, and we left without leaving him the offered drugs and apparently not wiser than before this excursion to the lower depths.

The next day at noon, I was sitting outdoors at Violeta's, eating their cheese- and cabbage-strudel, when suddenly Titus appeared out of nowhere and sat down next to me. I ordered him a cremeş. How he came to know it, I don't know, but he, like almost all of Timişoara, knew about my trip to Ronaţ, "I am pleased to see you are still in one piece. I understand you paid a visit to Timişoara's best known necrophiliac. Is it true he is on drugs these days?"

As if on autopilot, we both ended up smiling at these macabre facts of life. I gave Titus a brief run-down of Petrescu's words.

"Have you talked it over with Traian yet?"

"Why Traian?" I asked surprised. How would he know Petrescu? He was not even in the Party.

"True, he was not. I was, and he was not. Before that we both were your friends and now again we both are your friends. Yet, one of us has behaved more honorably than the other."

"Categories like honor lose their meaning under certain conditions, and you must admit that the Ceauşescu period met those conditions." I tried to defuse this explosive issue.

"I wouldn't go as far as saying that they lose their meaning, I'd rather say their meaning gets deformed. Remember T who lived on the Tudor Vladimirescu Quay, next to the U's who tried to escape to the West through Serbia, but were caught along with X...." I stopped listening and whatever content there was in Titus' lecture on totalitarian ethics and morals went lost. Much, much later did I only begin to understand the true extent of this loss.

That evening, Titus' question started resonating in my mind, "Have you talked it over with Traian yet?" Does Traian know something about Petrescu? Was Petrescu an opera-fan as well, an admirer of Scarpia's torturing Cavaradossi and Tosca? Why would both these *Securitate* heavies befriend a man who refused to join the Party? Did Traian know more about the parchment than he let on so far? I had to find out. So, the very next day I paid Traian a visit. Both he and Rodica, his effusive wife, were happy to see me, and on this warm and humid morning offered me homemade elderberry juice. It was just gently cooled so its subtle flavor could be tasted in full.

Like Titus, so also the Mărgineanus had heard of my trip to the Ronaţ hell. I asked them whether they had ever met Petrescu. Impulsive Rodica jumped in with an answer, "Sure, we had the opportunity to meet that monster and his boss when they were still riding high. Traian saw them at least, what would you say...." She looked at her husband who was visibly annoyed by this remark, and she switched off into silence. Without missing one beat, Traian asked her "How about some more juice for our friend." When Rodica took the cue, he went on, "Yes, when I went to listen to *Il Trovatore* with Grigorescu, then this Petrescu fellow had also joined us, and after Count Luna had his own brother burned to death, Petrescu insisted on giving me a tour of the Loga Row torture chambers. It was both horrifying and scary, horrifying because of the immense pain on view, scary because Petrescu made it perfectly clear that even I and my family could be brought in if they felt like it. It was all said with tongue in cheek, but clearly visible brute force was pushing the tongue uncomfortably in the cheek. It came off more as a threat than as a joke. I don't remember any substantive discussion with this man. Thank God, I must add."

"How did Mirela's boy end up there?"

"How would I know?" A smiling Rodica reappeared from the kitchen and poured me more elderberry juice, "Take some more juice, you like it and it's good for you. It has lots of Vitamin N"

"Vitamin E" Traian corrected her.

"I think it's N!" the lady of the house insisted.

"There is no such thing." Traian almost shouted. Rodica gave a look begging me to support her, I raised my shoulders, indicating I know nothing about vitamins, I just happened to like elderberry juice.

"The main thing is Petrescu did not bite you, and thus according to my Rodica missed his daily recommended dose of vitamin N."

It was clear that nothing more could be learned from the Mărgineanus. I looked at my watch and said I had to go. On the way back to the center of the city, I booked all this to Traian's honorable posture during those horrible years. I guess, there must be some truth to Titus' observation that honor does not completely lose its meaning even in the worst of times.

As to the parchment, the true cause of my current journey to Romania, I was as confused as before all these macabre visits. I started flirting with the idea that it was time to pack up my things and head back to the States. Yet in a rumor-filled place like Timişoara, all these visits had a beneficial side: people who could shed some light on any issue also hear the rumors, and hope for a pleasing reward then makes them step forward. To my mind, this was the only reason for which, not more than three hours after all that vitamin N tasting at Traian's house, I got an unexpected visit from a young man with a limp left arm,

"I am Dorel Costin, Mirela Costin's son."

"The one who had been detained at Loga Row by Grigorescu?"

"The very one. My mother, I understand you knew her, died due to the malpractice of a crazy surgeon."

"I am sorry, I have heard about that,"

"They did not prosecute, for that surgeon was a Party member. I guess his craziness allowed him to be one of the few true believers in Party dogma. Anyway, I came, for they say you want to know about that parchment. My arrest had to do with it, and my mother had told me a lot about it, about you. I had seen the damn thing many times before my arrest. I can still reproduce that map anytime, anywhere, you could say I know it by heart. Your ancestor's drawing is very accurate. I can tell, because I did go once to Alba Iulia where he buried all those things. The map locates the Catholic church, the synagogue and the fortress perfectly. A professional cartographer could not have done a better job. But then the buried "treasure," pardon me for using this exaggeration, should be easy to locate, except it cannot be where it is drawn, for at that very spot is City Hall, and this building dates back to the eighteenth century and therefore had to have been standing there already at the time your ancestor stopped in the city of Gyulafehérvár, as Alba Iulia was known then. He probably drew the map from memory, many years later and must have misremembered some details. I understand that Petrescu and Grigorescu also went there and also did not find anything. It's all as if Abbé Faria in *The Count of Monte Cristo* had been suffering of the early symptoms of Alzheimer's disease, when he directed Edmond Dantès to his treasure.

"That all sounds very interesting. Could you all the same draw that famous map for me?"

"It would give me pleasure, great pleasure." From my bag I produced a sheet of paper and Dorel Costin started drawing, fortunately he was right-handed. He drew fast, he obviously had done this so many times before, that he had no need to think, the lines and dots jumped into their places and his hand was merely following the orders it received from them.

Then he put the pencil down, took a last look at what he had drawn and with some satisfaction said "This is about it." The big dot where City Hall stands is clearly the treasure's place, but as I told you that is impossible, so this map is a wonderful introduction to the marvels of Alba Iulia, but hardly anything of any real value to anyone."

"What are these other two points?" I asked him when I noticed two point-like objects on the sheet of paper.

"That is a very good question. I had asked it too. I even went there and found nothing remarkable at either of them. I did some digging at both, but to no avail."

"Why did Grigorescu have you arrested?"

"He thought I may have tampered with the map, or maybe even have dug up the treasure myself. I paid dearly for Grigorescu's suspicions" he threw an anger-filled look at his lame left arm. Then he looked at the floor and with a clear degree of finality intoned the words "It's quite hot today, wouldn't you say so? Is it that hot in America as well?"

It was clear that Dorel Costin had provided all he knew about the parchment. I wanted to somehow thank him and invited him to a charming little restaurant near the County Hospital. It had an outdoor garden around a small man-made pond. There, over some drinks and delicious Szeged fish-soup, he, with a somewhat embarrassed timid smile and a bout of nervous coughing, baring his cavity-filled teeth, asked me about my relationship with his mother. I reciprocated his smile and said nothing. Then in a barely audible voice, somewhat horse from the coughing, he asked me, "Were you her first?"

Fearing this question, I kept my smile intact, and held on to my silence. Dorel correctly interpreted this as an affirmative answer. He questioningly raised his eyes for a second, and then with resignation started nodding. That very moment the waiter brought the apricot *crêpes à l'hongroise*, and after a sweet wine we got up in silence and took our leave.

I was now finally in possession of the map, or at least of a supposedly faithful replica thereof. I packed a small suitcase with clothes for a brief trip, went out to the taxi station next to the Philharmonic's beautiful, if dilapidated, art deco hall, and instructed the driver to head for Alba Iulia. The man reacted as if he had hit the jackpot, and proudly made some phone calls to his central and to some friends. All these calls seemed to address personal issues, until he kept throwing in at some point something like "Yes, I am on my way to Alba...." omitting an "eat your heart out" which he had tried to convey in a quite understandable fashion through the tone of his previous words. Within the hour, the Timişoara rumor mill was churning out reports about my departure for Alba Iulia. When I next checked my email, there were messages from Titus, from Traian, from Grigorescu and a few others wishing me a pleasant stay in that old fortress city.

I spent my first evening walking around this small but exquisite town. The fortress, as its name implies is white, a sign of good moral posture in the days of yore. Two men, one middle-aged and afflicted by a mild limp, the other young and spritely were clearly tailing me, aware of each other but not together. To assess the situation as correctly as I could, I doubled the speed of my walk, and just as I expected, so did my two shadows. So say, one is Grigorescu's man, then who is the other one? No, neither Traian, nor Titus would stoop to this. Petrescu? He didn't even bother to send me an email message. Well, I'll get to see that later. After having seen the fortress, the Catholic church and the synagogue, I made a sudden turn and headed back to my hotel. Dorel was right, these three landmarks were very accurately rendered in my ancestor's drawing, but I still couldn't understand those other two points.

Back in my room, I kept staring at the map. I noticed a small line almost a point itself, where on site I remembered having seen a tall fir tree. A new triangle, the "other-tree" triangle as I started calling it, with this tree, and the mysterious two "other" points as its vertices looked very familiar. Yes, no doubt, it was congruent to the "basic" Catholic-church-fortress-City-Hall triangle, which omitted as irrelevant the synagogue. But to an orthodox Jew like my ancestor the synagogue would have been a crucial sign-post on his map. As it was, the synagogue stood quite precisely at the center of this basic triangle. Suddenly it all became clear to me, the treasure had to be buried at the center of the other-tree triangle. It was not marked on the map, but then important things are subtle and can only be seen by those who understand their hidden meaning. "It was in code, the whole parchment and even the map," in the words of the old Jews murdered by Petrescu Such a reasoning was beyond the capacities of a *Securitate* torturer, or of a *Securitate* torturer's boss, or even of a decent limp-armed boy educated in a school in which religion and its accoutrements were seen merely as opiate for the people. I decided to take a walk in the morning to see whether this geometric reasoning had any merit.

I switched off the lights and wanted to call it a day, but I was excited and a full moon lit my room. I had a hard time falling asleep, but sometime around midnight I fell in Morpheus' arms.

The next morning I went for a walk and traced out the other-tree triangle. It was easily manageable, its longest side was barely fifty yards, if that much. This triangle lay in its entirety in a park, and so its center could be found quite accurately by simply walking in the grass as if bent on relaxation. I did so, and stopped three times at random points to confuse my shadows. Finally, I lay down in the grass at one of these random points and closed my eyes. For all appearances, I was sound asleep. When I "woke up," and reopened my eyes, my two shadows were both gone, obviously respectful of another fellow's sleep.

From here on, the question became one of digging at the geometrically determined spot without being detected by the two shadows and without being caught by the authorities and arrested for violating some city ordinance or other. There was no way I could do this by myself, I needed help. In view of the doubts that had arisen about both Titus and Traian, I thought it best not to rely on friends, and to hire a professional instead. But where would I find a person who could properly appreciate the cloak and dagger nature of this job? The more I thought about it, the clearer it became to me that this called for Sabin Spătaru, my very own Sam Spade. I called this Timişoara private eye who had already proved himself by getting me the parchment from Grigorescu. Without giving away anything about what I wanted him to do, I just offered him a three thousand Euro retainer for starters, and based on my earlier experience with him, I was sure this would bring him to Alba Iulia. It did. I also demanded complete discretion, complete silence, especially where the Ciocârlie brothers Cezar and Camil were concerned, but more generally I did not want this news spreading all over Timişoara. He said he understood and would be off the very next morning.

Upon his arrival, I asked him to get me two able-bodied men to dig up a spot in a park, preferably in the middle of the night.

"And for that you made me come to this faraway place?"

"Yes, I want you to find me these diggers and then supervise them while I walk around aimlessly to confuse my two shadows."

"Why *two* shadows?"

"I too have been thinking about that question ever since my arrival."

"One guy must be Grigorescu's man. For such jobs he employs this fellow with a limp. He got his limp at Petrescu's hands. They were playing good-cop-bad-cop with him, and Grigorescu cast himself as the good cop. He played this role so successfully, that the guy, out of gratitude I guess, is working for him to this day."

"I also figured that one of the men must be working for Grigorescu, and now I know which one, for one of the men does indeed have a limp. But that leaves the other fellow."

"Petrescu wouldn't have sent him. Nah! You saw what he is like these days, but some other party is obviously also interested in your doings here. I would just have to get my hands on this other shadow's mobile phone for a few minutes — that's easy, no problem — and I could tell you whom he is calling. Want me to?"

"That would be interesting, indeed, but let's not lose sight of what we really want to accomplish here. Later maybe?"

"Your call, really. Keep in mind that I can get you the two diggers in one hour at the most, and then we have the whole afternoon to wait for the arrival of darkness. Finding out who the other guy is would be fun, and I would do it for free as an extra for a good client." At this he started laughing loudly and this must have made him swallow the wrong way, so he was convulsed by an intense cough. At first I raised my shoulders but then ended up nodding. We shook on it, it was a deal.

In less than an hour, Spătaru had lined up two young skinheads willing to engage in nocturnal digging. With diggers at the ready, it now came down to the identity of the other shadow. It was part of Spătaru's professionally necessary anonymity that few people ever knew who he was, he blended in. This way, when he sat down at a table in the Carpaţi Café, nobody would have assumed that we knew each other. My two shadows also claimed one table each. Without saying anything to Spătaru, I first walked by the limping shadow's table. This elicited a smile from the detective. Then, pretending to be looking for the men's room, I passed the other shadow's table and stopped by it so suddenly, this man's face contorted in fear, he seemed to think I was about to hit him. I quickly asked a passing waiter, who then pointed with his arm in the direction I had to go. This time Spătaru's smile grew into what almost became a bout of laughter. The main task had been accomplished, Humphrey Bogart had taken cognizance of Peter Lorre. The rest was now his job.

Upon my return from the toilet all three men were still sitting in their old places. As I headed for the Café's door, Grigorescu's limping toady was the first to stand up and keep following me. Less than a minute later the other two rose almost simultaneously and the ranks of my followers were swelling as if I had turned into some latter day messiah. As ironic as it often can be, happenstance had me walking towards the synagogue's block. I stopped in front of this house of prayer noticed already by my distant ancestor, and decided to enter it. The limping guy, noticing this was some church-like building, instinctively if inappropriately removed his hat before also entering the building. The other two members of our platoon never came to pray. We could hear quite clearly why. They had been joined by Spătaru's nocturnal diggers, the two skinheads, loudly shouting swearwords at the unknown shadow, whom they kept calling "faggot" and accusing of having solicited sex from them. In no time at all, the confrontation became physical. Even standing near the synagogue's ark I could hear the muffled sound of human bodily force exerting human will on a weaker stranger. With the synagogue door closed we clearly heard a metallic object fall and then one of the skinheads shouting to his buddy

"What did the faggot throw away? His box of condoms?"

The other skinhead taking his time apparently to pick up the metallic object, then laughingly responded

"It's his mobile phone. Let's call his missus and tell her what he's up to. This must be it, all his calls are to this number" and he began shouting loudly a phone number starting with 256 the area code of Timişoara. I tried to memorize it, even though I was not sure I heard each digit clearly. Anyway, Spătaru must have jotted it down.

At this point I decided to leave the synagogue. On the street, the skinheads were gone, as was Sam Spade. All there was left was poor Peter Lorre, adjusting his mussed brown hair and then seeing whether the mobile phone, which the skinheads had apparently returned to him before running away, was still functional. He dialed, presumably the number recited by his attackers, and in a perfect monotone left a message of which I missed only a few words here and there,

"Lost the American. He went to a temple and outside .... mugged by two skinheads who thought ... queer. *I queer!* Can you imagine that?" Even this bigotedly phrased outrage did not break the monotone. "They roughed me up a little, but then they must have heard something, because very suddenly they ran away, both of them, and didn't even take my mobile phone, with which they could have made some expensive calls to Africa or Asia or wherever they were coming from." Obviously this shadow assumed that all dwellers in distant continents were still white and could only be distinguished from Europeans by the way they shaved their heads. As always, stupidity was bigotry's handmaiden.

I headed back to my hotel without any followers at all. Peter Lorre was sufficiently shaken up by the mugging, that he must have decided to take a rest, whereas Grigorescu's limping shadow had left the scene as soon as we made our exit from the temple. Barely had I arrived to my room, that on my mobile phone Spătaru was confirming that, "The number is neither Grigorescu's, of course, nor Petrescu's but it is the land-line of a yet to be identified private party. Complicated, huh?" Was it Traian, or maybe Titus, or who else?

With all these goings on, evening was falling and digging in the dark was the next task. On the way back to the hotel, it had started to rain.

Everything was wet now, and a cold haze covered the ground. At ten o'clock we met just inside the park by the main entrance. It was deserted. The two skinheads were there in a good mood. They laughed off the afternoon's confrontation. They were joyous, they were young, for them everything was a joke, an adventure. They found the staged mugging an inspired idea and were lavishing praise on Spătaru who had thought it all up. To someone who first met them in this embodiment, they could easily have passed for a pair of nice kids, but like most kids hereabouts they were not above selling their innocence for the right price.

For the first time I directed my three aides to the spot I by now knew how to reach taking seventeen steps from a big old chestnut tree. The two boys, each armed with a big shovel, started to dig. Spătaru and I were eagerly watching them. Spătaru was rubbing his hands, "It's cool tonight, and this haze…But then for our purposes that is just fine." I managed to step into a puddle and my feet were soaked, but excitement was still the dominant feeling I can recall. By now the skinheads were waist-deep in their holes, it looked like they were digging a grave. Yet there was no sign whatsoever of any "treasure." Spătaru looked at me as if I were a kook, a crackpot. I lowered my eyes and suggested the boys extend their digging a few feet in the direction of the chestnut tree. They grumbled but did as ordered.

At this very moment we heard a noise, someone was approaching us along the park's path. We halted all activity, hoping whoever is coming will pass without even noticing us. Suddenly the noise was getting very close, it was not human, it was a dog, wagging its short tail, happy for some company and maybe some food. Spătaru had brought a sausage along and he threw it to the dog. The animal devoured it fast, it was ravenous. Then it came back for more and gratefully licked the hand that had fed it. When it became clear to this dog that there was no more food to be had here, it ran on its way.

The boys resumed their digging and in no time at all one of them hit a metal object. All of us focused in on it. Quickly it was retrieved and the wet earth wiped off its surface. It was a quite badly rusted metal box, tin most likely, the size of an attaché case. It was handed to me and I opened it without difficulty. The thought momentarily crossed my mind, that Humphrey Bogart and the skinheads may now turn on me and mug me as they had mugged Peter Lorre hours earlier, but I needn't have worried, this Sam

Spade adhered to adequate professional standards, where his clients were concerned.

For better or worse, I opened my box and there they were, two small leather boxes containing the three rings, and a hardcover notebook somewhat dog-eared by centuries of humidity. With the help of Spătaru's strong flashlight, I recognized in this notebook on finest velum my ancestor's calligraphic handwriting. It seemed to be telling a story. We all agreed that reading that story was best done back at my hotel. For the time being Spătaru ordered the skinheads to fill the holes with the earth they had dug up. This went fast, and in less than half an hour we were leaving this geometrically special place. Spătaru handed one hundred Euros to each skinhead and I doubled these amounts. The two, actually quite nice boys became very loud in their gratitude, as if they had suddenly been transported to the serenade scene in the first act of *The Barber of Seville*. We thanked them and each of us headed his way.

At the hotel I immediately started going over my treasure. The rings were there, two wedding rings with names carved in Hebrew: Abraham and Rivka. That worked out right because in our family the men in alternating generations were Abrahams and Yossefs. My father was a Yossef and I am an Abraham. It then stands to reason that my great-great great-grandfather's father should have been an Abraham. The two-carat solitaire was beautiful and I could see the warm candle-lights of festive ballrooms in which this ring would have sparkled and highlighted the beauty of a crinoline-wearing lady's little hands. It was not of great value, for the stone was cut the old-fashioned way, no longer favored in modern times. Yet for me it had the value of something utterly personal: this ring must have already been worn by an ancestor of mine in the pre-crinoline days of the Napoleonic wars, in the days when dresses stressed the beauty of slim and tall women.

I put the rings away and took out the notebook. It was in Gothic handwriting as could have been predicted and it concerned precisely those Napoleonic times. When Bonaparte's troops headed for Moscow through my ancestors' shtetl, it was known that their *Empereur* was friendlier and fairer to the Jews than our Kaiser. Joshua, a leader of the local Jewry looked at Napoleon as a kind of messiah and decided to openly collaborate with the French. Others even joined Napoleon's army on its march East.

By contrast, a still sizable segment of the Jewish population remained loyal to the Kaiser.

Leah, a very beautiful woman lived in this shtetl. Though trying to remain totally apolitical, even this beauty was forced to make a choice. With many of her former lovers gone with the French troops, she set her eyes on a certain Chevalier Fabre de la Betouille, the French captain in charge of her shtetl and of a few neighboring ones. Here I cannot resist quoting the exact words of the notebook.

"This Fabre de la Betouille, a tall blond fellow with a mustache, came to our shtetl every other day. He was to make sure the route along which provisions were shipped to the troops in the East could be counted on as being safe. He showed up on the first day of Shevuoth, and on account of the religious rites being observed that day, had to remain with us overnight. It was decided that he be quartered in Leah's house. Given this woman's reputation, no one saw anything untoward in this decision. It all seemed to have gone very well, for after that night, the Captain moved his headquarters to Leah's house. It appeared that in her own apolitical way, Leah had also become a helper of the French.

People started shunning Leah, and in retaliation, as it were, she kept passing on to her mustachioed lover the gossip she could still overhear during the day. This led to a number of arrests of Jewish Kaiser-loyalists. One of them was even executed on the shtetl's main square, he had apparently wanted to set fire to the big granary full with flour for the French troops. People were stunned, but no one suspected the beauty, what did she understand of politics? The rebbe was convinced the French had planted disguised informers in the Jewish population.

Ostracized, Leah wanted to join the ranks of those who openly worked for the French, but the Chevalier induced her not to do this, for he found her much more useful, wearing the white cap of the apolitical person. They say this Chevalier had fallen in love with Leah. Was she in love with him as well? It would have been a first for her. Though those who had made love to Leah were plentiful, those she loved were few if any.

It was this Leah, some ten years later who first inducted me in the sublime world of the pleasures of the flesh. She had treated me with the condescension an elderly woman directs at a *yeled*, an almost child. I remember how nervous I had been the first time, but how on the second and the third and the next and next times, when I no longer had anything to prove to this slightly fading beauty, I felt a pleasure so great and so marvelously powered by a feeling of complete and uniform tension extending over the whole of my body, that I was rendered happy, as never before.

Her love for me was akin to mother's love, and like a mother who trusts her child, this Leah told me about her great love for the Chevalier. By then the war was long over, and people were no longer filled with hatred for those who had helped the French. Yet when they mentioned one or another of these figures who had compromised themselves, they made sure to attach to their names a smile that by its very shape measured the disdain in which they held the person referred to. They would talk differently of Joshua, than they would talk of Leah. Joshua, now a devoted servant of our Kaiser for a change, had made a fortune in his office, dealing with the French. On the other hand, Leah had experienced true ecstasy in her bed loving her Chevalier. They found her the more honorable of the two, even though she was no more than a weak woman. In the worst of circumstances one can still speak of honor, and when it came to honor, as far as the Jews of our *shtetl* were concerned, Leah carried the day, even though her Chevalier had been a goy."

It was uncanny, how the same topics involving that same shapeless concept of honor arise in the Bukovina of the Napoleonic wars with the same intensity as in Ceauşescu's Romania during the Cold War. Maybe my family is carrying a heredity that makes it susceptible to this topic. But beyond this ancestor of mine and myself, also Titus and in his own way Traian are dealing with this same issue. In today's world the American sense of pragmatism has chased honor out of public discourse. Compromise is now the order of the day. But those trying to make ends meet by the river Bega's muddy waters, cannot afford to be pragmatic, for the river's very waterbed is made of soft and slimy mud, and only by invoking the murky concept of honor can they gain a footing.

I was simply overwhelmed by the closeness between my calligraphically distinguished ancestor's preoccupations and my own. His description of the notebook as "a document of great value to my descendents" was nothing short of prophetic. .

I started thinking of all these ideas, and what with all the events of the day, I suddenly felt very tired, put the notebook down, and decided to go to sleep and then read the rest in the morning.

It was anything but a peaceful night. Shortly after the ringing-in of midnight on the city's numerous and poorly synchronized church-bells, I could hear footsteps in the corridor outside my room. These steps came to a halt in front of my room's door. Someone was trying to pry that door open. I rose in the bed and took the bottle of mineral water from my night-table in my hand, ready to break it against the bed frame and use it as a weapon. The first thing that came to my mind was the name Grigorescu. This made all the more sense since the footsteps were those of two persons, one Haydnesquely regular and the other in a limping man's Schumannesque dotted rhythm. How greedy can this torturer be, if he has to resort to third and fourth party theft or even murder in order to acquire three rings of no particular value? But then, who knows what fantasies were running in the soap factory executive's mind. I could just hear him quoting by heart excerpts from the *Protocols of the Elders of Zion*, and actually believing all that preposterous nonsense concocted by some czarist secret policeman or other.

After a bit of thinking, I decided that my best course of action was to make the men at my door know I am awake and ready to use force on them. I coughed, I turned on the light and started to speak into my mobile phone, loud enough for them to be able to hear my every word,

"Yes, and make sure to bring also the two skinheads. Give them the guns you bought and tell them to shoot before asking any questions. So, when can you get here? ..... Ten minutes? That's fine. Let's teach them a lesson!"

After this ominous series of threats the attempt at prying my door open came to a halt and a bout of whispering started still in front of the door. These would-be burglars did not even take the precaution of withdrawing a bit, lest I catch wind of their plans. Actually I could only hear every third or fourth word, but they had no way of knowing that. The one word that kept being repeated was Grigorescu's name, but that only confirmed what I was sure of anyway.

From the hotel phone on my night-table, I now dialed my mobile phone. I picked up after two rings and scared the daylights out of my would-be assailants,

"Where are you? .... At the corner? Run up to my room and don't wait, just start shooting." This line had the desired effect, for I could hear both Haydn and Schumann running for their lives.

Once alone, and in no danger any longer, in spite of the late hour, I dialed Spătaru's mobile. It took five rings before he picked up and in a yawning voice asked me what I wanted at this time of the night. I told him what had just happened, and this elicited a chuckle from Sam Spade, "Don't worry, the limping guy and whoever it was that came with him would not have shot you. These are Grigorescu's men, and for them valor amounts to putting out a cigarette in someone's cheek, not shooting him point blank. They know that you have found something, maybe they followed you to the park and didn't dare approach us because of the presence of the boys. They were just literally trying to save face, for if they came back completely without any clue about what you found, Grigorescu may extinguish his cigarette on *their* cheeks. By the way, I wonder who the other fellow was. What do you want to do now?"

"Leave as soon as I can, but how?"

"That's no problem. Let me rest till five in the morning, then I come to pick you up at the hotel and I will drive you back to Timişoara, myself. That way you'll be safe. Is that fine?"

"That is fine indeed. Thanks!"

I was due for a good rest myself, but I just couldn't relax enough to fall asleep. I picked up the notebook and continued my reading. It wasn't easy at this point to decipher all those beautiful Gothic letters with all their curlicues, but somehow I managed.

Ominously, my ancestor introduced a new set of characters in his story, the mostly Ukrainian inhabitants of two villages close to his shtetl. These Ukrainians hated the French, they hated the Austrians and the Hungarians, and above all they hated the Jews, whom they viewed as "Murderers of the Christ." Ostensibly bent on punishing the Jews for having helped that evil Napoleon, they started staging a series of pogroms. On the third day of their pogrom week they got to my ancestor's shtetl and with fire and sword murdered, pillaged and destroyed. In his own words,

"In the middle of the night, some fifty men from around Sadhora entered our shtetl and headed for the main square. There they demanded to be handed over Leah, whom they kept calling 'the Frenchman's whore of Babylon' and whom they wanted to burn at the stake. Facing these armed Ukraininas, were standing all the Jewish men of our shtetl, wearing yarmulkes many fingering their rich forelocks. 'No' was our collective one-word reply. This negative word was then being used as an excuse to start the shooting. All fifty Ukrainians were carrying guns and all started shooting at the Jews, something they must have dreamt of doing at many times in their lives. All around me, the unarmed Jews were falling inanimately. As if ordered, I also fell, though I had not been hit. I lay there without moving while the Ukrainians moved on to set fire to our houses.

When they finally left, I got up. There were some ten of us unhurt. We took cognizance of each other with painful smiles, a natural reaction for survivors of such a horror. Somehow I did not feel like talking to anyone. I just went down to the brook flowing through the shtetl and started thinking. It suddenly became clear to me that I had to move to a place where the Jew can live safely in peace, where he can defend himself against murderers bent on doing away with him. The Jew should no longer live by the law of the Austrian, of the French, of the Hungarian or Ukrainian, but by the law of the Jew. Where in the world is there such a place I asked myself. It became clear to me that such a place does not exist. In the mean time what could I do? I had once heard that there is this city called Temesvar where the word 'pogrom' is unknown, and I decided to get my things together still that day and leave for Temesvar."

I finally understood what had brought my family to Temesvar. It had been a combination of a Jew fleeing from vicious murderers, and his understanding of some ideas not yet known in his day, ideas that in the distant future would be put forward by a Hungarian Jew, a distinguished journalist in Vienna. As foreseen by my ancestor, this cast a completely new light on my heritage.

At five sharp, Spătaru's Skoda stopped in front of my hotel. I jumped in and at this early hour Sam Spade could speed toward the city on the Bega. He asked me what I had found out from the notebook. I told him about Napoleon and about Leah. That made a big impression, for in Timişoara to the present day that emperor is still revered as if he had won the battle at Waterloo. I left out the Zionist intimations, those are not for Sam Spade. In the early nineteenth century they were no more than the "Stuff that dreams were made of."

"I thought all along that you expected too much from that ledger" the detective told me. "You wasted all that money. Was it worth it? I doubt it, but now even you know it wasn't and that is what matters after all." I nodded and finally managed to fall asleep.

Spătaru drove me directly to my hotel, by the river. I got out and in my room I immediately went back to sleep. I remember I had vivid dreams. I was in a village next to Timişoara and even around here they had heard the word pogrom. Swabian, Hungarian and Romanian peasants decked out in their national attire wanted to burn me at the stake. The other Jews were prodding me to submit, lest the pogrom become all-encompassing. They started pushing me toward a tall and fat Swabian peasant who devil-like wanted to lift me on his pitchfork. He was complaining to his Hungarian buddy that not a single Serbian peasant had joined the pogrom party. The Hungarian replied "Yes, the Serbians have yet to learn how one hates a Jew," and found his insight so funny, that he started laughing loudly. The other peasants joined him in his laughter. Just as the pitchfork came within a few feet from my chest, on the main road Humphrey Bogart and Sidney Greenstreet brought Spătaru's Skoda to a screechy halt and waved me in its back seat. They were going to speed away and thus rescue me, but it never got to that, for covered in sweat I woke up, my caged heart beating furiously in my heaving chest.

My phone was also ringing. It was Grigorescu,

"I heard you found something. You will agree that I have a right to see what you found and share in it. Without the parchment you had stolen from my office, you fucking Jew, you'd never have found a thing." I was not going to start my day on such insults and I hung up. The phone rang again, but I didn't pick up.

The only people I still had to speak to before leaving this city where the word pogrom had by now been spoken, but not too often, were Traian and Titus. To avoid being at the receiving end of further calls from Grigorescu, or even Petrescu, I had to call my two friends rather than wait to be called by them.

I dialed Traian's number from the hotel phone on my night table. Rodica answered,

"We've heard, you found the big diamond and that book with instructions of how to find the rest of the treasure. You'll end up filthy rich. Let me pass you Traian." They have heard, how was that possible? I had just returned hours earlier and Spătaru was not one to spread the news. Traian picked up,

"So that parchment was of use after all. I am glad I could be of help. Please do not misunderstand me, I do not claim a reward. My reward is that you have found what you were looking for." What was going on here? It is the oldest rhetorical trick to specify your demands by indicating what you supposedly do *not* ask for. Above all, how is it that they know so much about what was found in Alba Iulia. At this moment, my mobile started ringing and it had to be Spătaru. I told Traian I would drop in later at their place and hung up.

It was Sam Spade just as I had guessed,

"I checked on that number the boys got from the other guy in front of the Jewish church" an interesting way of putting it. "It is the land-line of a certain Titus Comloşan. Ring any bell?"

"Ring all the bells! So it was my good friend Titus." I can just hear him tell it. When you went to Alba, Sergiu, who lived in the Elizabethan district next to the Lahovari square, where Sári Néni used to be, told me he is also going to Alba and I asked him to keep an eye on you, just in case..... Yeah, precisely, just in case I find the "treasure." Being written with such calligraphic virtuosity, this parchment, after all these years, had acquired mythical proportions. For me it had a deep personal meaning, it threw some light on where I came from. For these people, be they Ceauşescu's torturers or his victims this was a treasure, it was their ticket to well-being. But it still did not add up. Grigorescu's limping cowboy was understandable, but Titus' man roughed up by the boys was still wrapped in a thick shroud of mystery.

I had to get to the bottom of this business. What did all these people want from me? What motivated them to go to these lengths to know my every step?

I jumped into a cab and had the driver take me to the Mărgineanus' place. Traian received me at the front door with his routine embrace and ear-to-ear smile. Rodica ran to the kitchen and brought the jug of elderberry juice, "Drink it, it's good for you, vitamin X." We all laughed, and I found this weird. Somehow in this city everything leads either to a smile or to a bout of laughter, as if people had forgotten how to cry.

I had brought along the notebook and the three rings. Longingly and admiringly they examined the diamond, and asked me whether the notebook contains directions for finding the rest of the treasure. I decided to disabuse them of these get-rich-quick fantasies, "What you see is all there is." They exchanged you-can't-fool-us looks and then started staring at me expecting me to reveal the formula, the "Open Sesame" with which they could also get themselves a share. I shouted at Traian, "There is no treasure island hidden anywhere, this is all there is, *basta*! My family is not related to Robert Louis Stevenson's." They looked dejected and it was clear they suspected me of holding out on them. But there was an equally, if not more, pressing point on my mind: I had to find out about the second shadow. So, I drastically changed the subject, "How did you know what I had found, how did you even know I had found anything at all?" They were not prepared for this question, and, taken by surprise, they did what most people would do, they became defensive,

"Are you accusing us of having you shadowed?"

"Not really. I was shadowed by a man sent by Grigorescu and another one sent by Titus. That's it, there was no third man. There is however the question of the precise nature of your relation to Grigorescu, which to say the least, has 'fluctuated' since its existence had been revealed. What can *you* tell me about it?"

The end of my question was punctuated by the sound of the front door bell. Rodica rushed to see who is there, and I could distinctly hear Titus' voice, speaking some three words and then being lowered to a faint whisper. Next, the door slammed and Rodica returned to the dining table at which we were sitting, "It was a neighbor asking if I had some yeast. He was out of luck, I have none." By this time I knew that the second man was reporting to Titus, but deformed honor or not, it was becoming clearer by the minute that the Mărgineanus were also involved somehow.

"Well, how about Grigorescu?" I quite impatiently repeated my question.

"I don't know what you mean."

"I mean that he had a man shadowing me in Alba, and so did Titus. At least one of these two men's reports has reached you as well, and since you supposedly have hardly any relationship with Titus, this leaves Grigorescu as your only source. I want to understand precisely the nature of your relation with Grigorescu. And please let's forget Fedora Barbieri."

"For heaven's sakes, it was me who spotted that parchment in Grigorescu's office, and you must admit that without it you could not have done anything. It had to be stolen from Grigorescu, without his realizing that anything was missing. How could you even think that I had what you have the gall to call, quite insultingly I must add, a relationship, or even worse that I was conspiring with that torturer."

"Please do not put words in my mouth, words I never uttered. I am certainly not into any conspiracy theories. On the other hand, how did you come to even think in terms of those words?" I was looking Traian in the eyes, quite accusingly. He lowered his head and said nothing. This gave me the opportunity to continue with my interrogation,

"Why was Dorel Costin arrested?"

"I told you I have no idea."

"I think you do and this is the right moment to tell me."

"It was something with that parchment."

"But how did Grigorescu even know of its existence?"

"Because Mirela kept talking about it."

"To whom did she talk about it?"

"To me, for instance!" Traian almost shouted.

"Because she trusted you. Did she talk to anyone else?"

"How would I know?"

"It is then possible that she had only talked to you, in which case I cannot but wonder how Grigorescu got the news."

"Are you implying that I told him?"

"I am not implying anything, I am just putting the facts together and drawing the obvious conclusions. Rodica, as you may recall, said you saw Grigorescu on many occasions."

"She was confused."

"I would say she was truthful. Look this does not seem to go anywhere. Why don't we stop here? I'll leave and if you have anything more to add, you know where to find me. Just, please, please do not send those guys who shadowed me in Alba." I got up and headed to the front door. Traian remained seated, he was like paralyzed, and appeared deeply in thought.

The sunny street was a welcome relief after the dark stuffed atmosphere of the Mărgineanu apartment. I called Titus and asked him to join me at Violeta's. Half an hour later, we were digging into our usual fares, I strudel and Titus cremeş. We also had some Borsec water and espressos to keep us alert.

"I wanted to see you, because you sent someone to spy on me in Alba. This someone together with another man sent by Grigorescu even tried to break into my hotel room and who knows what they would have done to me. That this man was sent by you is established beyond any doubt. His mobile phone had all its calls to you. I demand an explanation without your building one of your usual chains of names."

"What chains of names?"

"Never mind, just explain yourself, that's all. I, as your friend, have the right to ask this from you."

"Alright, shortly after I heard about your trip to Alba, Traian called me. He had also heard about it, as had Grigorescu, who had told Traian that he sent the limping fellow after you." My worst suspicions were being confirmed, but I did not dare interrupt Titus, lest he revert to his name chains.

"Traian was afraid the limping guy would mug you and steal anything you might have found. Both he and Grigorescu were convinced that you were searching for a vast fortune, and both felt they were entitled to a sizable share. So, Traian suggested I should hire someone to keep a tab on the limping guy. He would pay, but the man I hire would report to me, so as not to strain his relation to Grigorescu, should he find out what we were doing."

Here I could no longer master myself, I butted in, "What is this relationship between Traian and Grigorescu, that you are talking about?"

"Come on, you cannot be so naïve. Traian obstinately refused to join the party, even thought his career was destroyed for all practical purposes as a consequence of this obstinacy. Yet, even in the old days he never went wanting, they lived as well as one could in Ceauşescu's Romania. How do you think he did this? *He was an informer*, that's how, and the good life was his reward! Later on, he might have wanted to become a party member and advance in his job, but I am convinced that Grigorescu, his sponsor, would not allow this to happen. A good informer had to keep a low profile, unaffiliated with the party or the *Securitate*, otherwise he became obvious and as such useless. Remember Marin Popescu, who was at high school with us, the one who then moved to Arad, where he became a journalist at the party newspaper. Everyone knew he informed and he became so worthless that he was fired and had he not married Cecilia the daughter of the ....."

"Stop it! Please!" Titus knew only too well what he was doing, and my outrage at his behavior had him laugh out loud. I went on, "You are accusing Traian of having been an informer. Do you have any evidence whatsoever for this horrible accusation, or are you simply yielding to your visceral dislike of Traian?"

Titus looked me straight in the eyes, and then, his mouth quivering with a combination of anger and triumphalism, started playing his trump card, "Mirela told me about your parchment."

"She told you too? I wonder to how many others she may have told."

"Just wait, don't interrupt me. In those days Traian was my unquestionable hero, so next time I saw him, *I* told *him* what I had learned from Mirela. He had never heard about the parchment and was very, very interested. He asked me many questions. A week later Dorel Costin was arrested and tortured as only that motherfucker and his henchman Petrescu knew how. In no time at all Mirela surrendered the parchment to Grigorescu. It is then that I became sure that Traian was an informer."

"But you and Traian hired that man for the Alba job together. As I told you already, he and Grigorescu's limping cowboy, the two of them jointly, tried to break in to my hotel room in Alba. How do you explain that?"

"It may sound self-serving, but when Traian suggested I hire that man to shadow you, I went along for two reasons. On the one hand, I wanted to see you protected, what with someone hired by Grigorescu tailing you, you may have ended up a cripple. But then, I must admit, I also had fantasies of striking it rich."

I thanked Titus for his frankness, an action that pleased him so much, he insisted on paying the tab. I did not accept and we compromised, we each paid half the bill.

I left the pastry shop totally confused. Titus had thrown at me a clear and consistent story, no doubt about that. By then I had my own doubts about Traian, and now Titus had confirmed these doubts without any prompting from me. But then, there are two or sometimes even more sides to every story. Is there a way for Traian to redeem himself? I couldn't see how, but I wanted to make sure I am not jumping the gun in demoting Traian from the high ground of moral rectitude to the gutter-side dwelling of the man who, for profit is willing to spy on and denounce even his best friend. As if jogging, I ran to the Mărgineanu residence.

Traian received me without his customary smile and without the familiar embrace. His face was covered with the wrinkles of fear and stress. He led me to the dining table. Rodica, walking slowly without the energetic eagerness of the one serving vitamin N, put out some crackers and a pitcher filled with unchilled tap-water. All three of us were sitting silently and rigidly stiff. It was a genuine still life.

"You know what Titus told me?" I finally asked.

"I can imagine. He held me responsible for Dorel Costin's arrest. He has been reproaching me that for ages. I don't know how Grigorescu learned about your parchment, but it was not from me. Of course, there is no way I can prove this to you, for even if Grigorescu were to swear to you that it wasn't me, there is no reason for you to believe him. All I can tell you is that for me that old story is over. I am extremely sorry for what happened to Dorel, but it was not my fault."

"And the fellow you put to watch me in Alba? That was not your idea either. You were not interested in getting a share in the 'treasure,' a 'sizable' share? And your sighting of the parchment in Grigorescu's office was also just visual acuity rather than some prearrangement with Grigorescu? Come on!"

"There is no convincingly believable way I can answer any of your questions. As long as the ugly answers linger in your mind, our friendship lies here in ruins, totally wrecked, and there is nothing you or I can do about it. I suggest you leave right now and if ever you feel that you can understand my situation, then please come back. You will be welcome, I can promise you that much. All that happened today will be moved to the grey region of the forgotten, without any trace of rancor. We do not have much time left on this earth either of us, but time is what both of us need." At this point Traian got up, and Rodica and I also rose in what to a stranger could easily have looked like slow motion.

Heavy-heartedly I was walking to my hotel. My exchange with Titus about honor came to mind,

"Categories like honor lose their meaning under certain conditions ..." I had emphasized to Titus, only to get that inscrutable reply, "I wouldn't go as far as saying that they lose their meaning, I'd rather say their meaning gets deformed."

What Traian had proposed a few minutes ago was for me to try to understand the specific way in which the meaning of his honor had been deformed. I don't know whether I am up to the task.

It seemed as if what I had come for to Timişoara had largely been taken care of. Yet, I could not get rid of a sense that something was badly amiss, or unfinished, or maybe outright shameful. I could not put my finger on what that was, but as is often the case in such situations, you decide you have something to do, and only long after you did it do you realize that what you did was nothing more than trying to cope with your deep malaise.

I chased away all thought of immediately returning to the States. I had also more than my fill of Traian and Titus and of the Loga row boys, Grigorescu and Petrescu. Satisfied though I was with my choice of Sam Spade, what bothered me was no longer a matter for a Humphrey Bogart either. Out of the blue the name of Dorel Costin came to mind. I wanted to thank him for his unselfish help. I thought it would be appropriate to give him a large share of the "treasure," after all without his map I would have found nothing. I did not want to part with the rings, as they were precious heirlooms, but I could maybe convince Dorel to accept a cash-offering instead, an offering intended not as a payment but as his well-deserved share.

On the spur of the moment I dialed his number. This took him by surprise, a pleasant surprise, judging by the tone of his voice. We agreed to meet for dinner at the restaurant near the County hospital, where he had asked me all those questions about Mirela.

They gave us the same table as before. Right away I showed him the rings. The wedding rings held no interest for him, but the solitaire's fire impressed him somewhat like the Big Macs impressed Russians at Moscow's first McDonald's when meat was scarce and therefore considered a major delicacy in the then still Soviet state.

I brought Dorel up to date on how I found the "treasure" and asked him to accept five thousand Euros as his share. He was visibly stunned but he neither accepted nor did he turn down my offer. Realizing that he could shed some light on the issue about Traian's behavior, I asked him,

"How in your opinion has Grigorescu come to know about the parchment?"

"Somebody had obviously told him" was his way of avoiding an answer to my question.

"What I should have asked you is whether you know or at least think you know who that was."

"Somebody who either wanted to ingratiate himself with that monster, or wanted to save his own imperiled skin. Why are you asking me at this late time? Do *you* know who it was?"

"I think I do, and it causes me a lot of pain, because it was someone whom I counted as a close friend, and now our friendship has unraveled."

"I think you must mean Mr. Traian Mărgineanu. I figured that out long ago, and held the man in deepest contempt. But then, after the fall of Ceauşescu he came to me. At first I refused to speak to him, but he just about begged me, so I listened to what he had to say. He admitted it was he who informed Grigorescu, while they were listening to the record of some opera or operetta. Then, he made it clear that he told Grigorescu about the parchment after that even more monstrous Petrescu had threatened him with the possibility of arresting and torturing him and his family. Anything one does under such a threat is forgivable. One faces a horrible choice. Should one destroy the lives of those one loves best, or the life of an innocent bystander? No matter what you choose, you end up hating yourself. I don't know whether you are aware, but Mr. Mărgineanu's career went nowhere, he was a total failure. It was not that he lacked talent. On the contrary, I understand that he was good at his profession. It was his way of punishing himself for what he had done to me. I cannot hate such a man. Ever since, Mr. Mărgineanu and I have kept up friendly relations. We are not close, but we respect each other. I find what he did acceptable, even honorable in the sick sense of those times. At the same time I find your self-righteous indignation not only misplaced, but dishonorable. You sat that whole nightmare out in comfortable America, and now you come here and judge us as if we were defendants in a court of law. Well, we are not!" Dorel Costin was looking intently at me and must have noticed my own unease at his words. He just about jumped up and said,

"On second thought, keep your money, Sir, I do not wish to get a share of what is rightfully yours. If I was of help, as you say, that is fine with me, but I do not wish to have anything to do with you, Sir. Goodbye!" At this he fast and forcefully left the restaurant.

CPSIA information can be obtained at www.ICGtesting.com
Printed in the USA
LVOW131716030812

292845LV00011B/102/P